MACABRE RAILWAY STORIES

The Age of Steam revolutionised not only the transport but the reading habits of the nation and with the latter came the increasing popularity of ghost stories and similar macabre tales. While progress and modernisation was taking place in all other directions this branch-line of literature seemed to be returning to superstition and the darkness of the Middle Ages.

Ronald Holmes has established a reputation as a writer on the macabre and as a collector of stories irresistible to those who enjoy the thrill of fear.

MACABRE RAILWAY STORIES

Compiled and edited by
Ronald Holmes

A STAR BOOK
published by
the Paperback Division of
W. H. ALLEN & Co. Ltd

A Star Book
Published in 1983
by the Paperback Division of
W. H. Allen & Co. Ltd
A Howard and Wyndham Company
44 Hill Street, London W1X 8LB

First published in Great Britain by W. H. Allen & Co. Ltd, 1982

Introduction and selection copyright © Ronald Holmes, 1982

Reproduced, printed and bound in Great Britain by
Hazell Watson & Viney Ltd, Aylesbury, Bucks

ISBN 0 352 31293 9

For
Valerie, Allan, Diane and Paul

CONTENTS

INTRODUCTION 7

THE SIGNALMAN 13
Charles Dickens

THE GARSIDE FELL DISASTER 29
L. T. C. Rolt

THE ENGINEER 41
Amelia B. Edwards

THE TUNNEL 63
Raymond Harvey

THE EIGHTH LAMP 75
Roy Vickers

THE COMPENSATION HOUSE 91
Charles Collins

ALL CHANGE 111
John Edgell

MIDNIGHT EXPRESS 119
A. Noyes

THE LAST TRAIN 127
Harry Harrison

THE TALE OF A GAS-LIGHT GHOST 135
Anonymous

THE ATTIC EXPRESS 149
Alex Hamilton

THE WOMAN IN THE GREEN DRESS   171
Joyce Marsh

THE VERY SILENT TRAVELLER   185
Paul Tabori

TAKE THE Z TRAIN   193
A. V. Harding

THE THIRD LEVEL   205
Jack Finney

THE MAN WHO RODE THE TRAINS   213
Paul A. Carter

ACKNOWLEDGEMENTS   233

INTRODUCTION

THIS COLLECTION OF macabre stories has been compiled specially for those who, besides enjoying the thrill of the supernatural, are interested in railways in general and steam-trains in particular—thus giving double pleasure to many readers. Nevertheless, each story stands in its own right as a work that will please and thrill the most discerning reader of macabre tales.

While researching this volume it soon became clear to me that the history of macabre stories and the steam-train coincided almost exactly; a very curious and interesting fact. Both saw an increase in popularity from about 1850 and reached a peak about 1900 that was followed by a decline. According to Hamilton Ellis, the years 'from the death of Queen Victoria to the outbreak of war were proud years. Enormous coal-trains rumbled and handsome expresses rushed about the country. Maintenance was high and locomotives were often painted in gorgeous colours.' Even railway publishing was at a peak—at this time *Bradshaw* ran to over eleven-hundred pages.

But there was more to be discovered. Not only did this similarity exist between the progress of the steam-train itself and macabre stories in general, but the same similarity existed in the case of the macabre railway story. I found it was possible to mark the events that lead up to the very first (in Britain, at least) railways' ghost story to be published. It all came about in the following way.

There were stories of the macabre published before 1850, of course, not the least of which were *The Castle of Otranto* and *Frankenstein*. These were mainly bound books too highly priced for the ordinary people of the time. But between 1820 and 1830, arising from the Industrial Revolution and the development of steam-power, both the rotary steam-press and machine-manufactured paper were introduced into publishing and it became possible for books, and particularly magazines, to be printed cheaply at a time when the literacy of the population was on the increase. Magazines such as *Blackwoods* and the *Cornhill* soon flourished and provided an avid reading public with the short stories and serials they demanded.

Very few of the various types of short story published during this period are remembered today. The striking exceptions are those ghost stories by Charles Dickens that are now regarded as classics—*A Christmas Carol* (1843), *The Chimes* (1844), *The Cricket on the Hearth* (1845) and many others. Dickens is said 'to have consolidated the modern taste and appreciation for the Supernatural story' and he certainly inspired and encouraged many other authors of the time to write stories in this manner.

His influence was greatly increased when, in 1850, he became the editor of *Household Words* and began to feature ghost stories in the Christmas editions of the magazine. As an editor he was able to commission stories and suggest plots to his authors and also, since it was an accepted editorial style of the time, arrange the stories of a particular issue to follow a set, common theme. This style is still used by anthologists today when considered appropriate and in the case of this book I believe I can do no better than to emulate Dickens himself.

In 1859, he closed down *Household Words* and opened up a new magazine entitled *All The Year Round*, and the theme he chose for the 1866 Christmas issue was a railway station called Mugby Junction. Many of the stories had little significance from a railway point of view, nor were they all ghost stories, but that edition did contain three ghost stories of a very high standard and I reprint these here to mark the origin of the Macabre Railway Story in Britain. Never before had the seemingly incompatible themes of the supernatural and the steam-train been brought together—and only a master could have brought it about.

Dickens' own contribution, *The Signalman*, has been

reprinted before but it is of such significance that I make no apology for printing it again here. The other two are less widely known, as is *The Tale of a Gas-light Ghost* reprinted from the *New Christmas Annual* of the following year.

Thus the Age of Steam revolutionised not only the transport but the reading habits of the nation and with the latter came the increasing popularity of ghost stories and similar macabre tales. Now this seems to be an inconsistency, a paradox, for while progress and modernisation was taking place in all other directions this branch-line of literature seemed to be returning to superstition and the darkness of the Middle Ages.

Other types of literature moved with the times. The forward-looking works of Jules Verne and, later, H. G. Wells were just as popular and stories of trips to the Moon and Mars appeared in *The Strand*. This seems consistent enough for these authors kept pace with, or slightly ahead of, the technical progress and speculation of the time. Why then, when science daily demonstrated the impossibility of vampires, ghosts and werewolves, did stories that took their existence for granted become more and more popular with the public?

It is true to say that this was a time of another great change. A revolution in the beliefs and faith of the people was also taking place. When we recall that, in 1879, the Bishop of Durham announced that the world was created at 9 a.m. on 23 October 4004 BC as some sort of answer to Darwin's *Origin of Species*, which had been published twenty years earlier, we begin to get some slight idea of the conflict between the material and spiritual concepts of life and thought that existed at the time. The old ways, the old beliefs, were being regarded as superstitions, but this did not make them disappear overnight and those people who still maintained the old values felt unhappy and insecure as the Industrial Revolution ushered in a new way of life and thought.

On examination, many early macabre stores can be seen to present a modern and enlightened situation at first, but up through the fabric of the story presses the magical relationships between man and his world, the old beliefs and values, the 'superstitions'. The story reflects the dilemma in the minds of many of the readers and comforts them by asserting the ultimate victory of goodness. In such stories the function of the ghost was to extract revenge, warn of danger, seek to right past evils or reveal secret hiding places. Ghosts, in the short story if not in fact, were the spiritual symbols of good as against evil or of right as against wrong—considerations that did not seem to have much significance in the new technological age—but that gave spiritual comfort to the reader while also supplying stimulating, enjoyable fear on the surface.

This was only true up until the end of the nineteenth century. As generation succeeded generation—both of readers and authors—the situation evolved through literary styles and plot constructions. Where the ghost had usually been a good or 'Christian' spirit the concept of an evil or 'pagan' spirit was introduced into short story plots and, since readers now required simple entertainment rather than spiritual comfort it did not matter a great deal whether good or evil triumphed in the end provided the story was a good one. If, as an example, we take the case of the successful film *Rosemary's Baby*, it would merely be necessary to change the last few feet of the film to completely reverse the ending from this point of view, but it would be just as effective and entertaining as before.

Although I have suggested that the popularity of the macabre story is past its peak it is not finished nor is it ever likely to be. The fact that you hold this book in your hand is proof enough. The peak occurred when every issue of Dickens' magazines (and others) were sold out immediately they were printed and each copy was read by an average of twenty people. Such things are of the past, together with the steam-train 'excursions' I still recall, bound for Belle Vue, Manchester, which ambled through every small station in Lancashire with people standing all the way.

In searching for suitable stories for this anthology I found that comparatively few good railway stories exist and only a very small proportion of them were of a macabre nature. My determination to include stories that were not only of high calibre but having also a high content of authentic railway settings and backgrounds made the task even more difficult. With regret I turned from *The Kill* by Peter Fleming (brother of Ian, the creator of James Bond), which is a really satisfying vampire story, because its only connection with railways is that it is set in a station waiting room. The superb .007 by Rudyard Kipling was set aside because, while it is replete with fantasy and whimsy, there is no hint of terror. I also considered those thrilling tales of Thorpe Hazell, the 'railway detective' by V. L. Whitechurch, with their wealth of technical railway detail (often supported by sketches of the lines, junctions and signalboxes) but these had to be set aside, alas, on the same grounds.

The stories I finally selected all have an atmosphere of steam, swaying cars and the disturbing rattle of wheels over the tracks. Disturbing too are the passengers—some skeletons, some corpses and even Death himself. So are the guards, the signalmen and the drivers. As far as possible, the stories have been chosen to cover the whole range of macabre railway stories from 1866 to the present day.

It is my most earnest request that readers do *not* read this book while travelling by rail. For when the train, screaming fearfully, hurtles into a dark, noisome tunnel, horror comes and the cold, skeletal hand of fear touches the nape of the neck and dark things press against the windows and scratch and scratch to get in.

Ronald Holmes
Broken Cross
Cheshire

THE SIGNALMAN

Charles Dickens

In June 1865, Charles Dickens was involved in a railway accident at Staplehurst, Kent. He was travelling in the South Eastern Railway's boat train from Folkestone when the train failed to stop at a bridge under repair. Dickens was in the first coach, and was lucky to escape with his life when it, together with the engine, ran across the rail-less bridge and was left hanging at a perilous angle. The experience affected his health and he avoided train travel for some time afterwards. The experience, he said was 'inexpressibly distressing'.

It seems reasonable to suppose that his thoughts turned to the possibility of premonition or 'spectral warning' of such railway accidents and from this beginning grew The Signalman, which was to be the basis for the 1866 Christmas issue of All the Year Round.

Although famous for his ghost stories, Dickens wrote only ten or eleven that can truly be called short stories since the remainder, The Chimes or A Christmas Carol, for example, were almost novel-length. Many of these were not published separately, but as a part of longer, often serialised, works such as Pickwick Papers or Nicholas Nickleby. This unusual treatment of one of his short stories of the supernatural, and the fact that it was the only one about railways, is significant in view of his almost premature death in a railway accident.

His readers knew nothing of this, but welcomed the excellent stories of, what was to them, the new and exciting wonder of the age—the steam engine.

'HALLOA! BELOW THERE!'

When he heard a voice thus calling to him, he was standing at the door of his box, with a flag in his hand, furled round its short pole. One would have thought, considering the nature of the ground, that he could not have doubted from what quarter the voice came; but, instead of looking up to where I stood on the top of the steep cutting nearly over his head, he turned himself about and looked down the Line. There was something remarkable in his manner of doing so, though I could not have said, for my life, what. But, I know it was remarkable enough to attract my notice, even though his figure was foreshortened and shadowed, down in the deep trench, and mine was high above him, so steeped in the glow of an angry sunset that I had shaded my eyes with my hand before I saw him at all.

'Halloa! Below!'

From looking down the Line, he turned himself about again, and, raising his eyes, saw my figure high above him.

'Is there any path by which I can come down and speak to you?'

He looked up at me without replying, and I looked down at him without pressing him too soon with a repetition of my idle question. Just then, there came a vague vibration in the earth and air, quickly changing into a violent pulsation, and an oncoming rush that caused me to start back, as though it had force to draw me down. When such vapour as rose to my height from this rapid train had passed me and was skimming away over the landscape, I looked down again, and saw him re-furling the flag he had shown while the train went by.

I repeated my inquiry. After a pause, during which he seemed to regard me with fixed attention, he motioned with his rolled-up flag towards a point on my level, some two or three hundred yards distant. I called down to him, 'All right!' and made for that point. There, by dint of looking closely about me, I found a rough zig-zag descending path notched out: which I followed.

The cutting was extremely deep, and unusually precipitate. It was made through a clammy stone that became oozier and wetter as I went down. For these reasons, I found the way long enough to give me time to recall a singular air of reluctance or compulsion with which he had pointed out the path.

When I came down low enough upon the zig-zag descent, to see him again, I saw that he was standing between the rails on the way by which the train had lately passed, in an attitude as if he were waiting for me to appear. He had his left hand at his chin, and that left elbow rested on his right hand crossed over his breast. His attitude was one of such expectation and watchfulness, that I stopped a moment, wondering at it.

I resumed my downward way, and, stepping out upon the level of the railroad and drawing nearer to him, saw that he was a dark sallow man, with a dark beard and rather heavy eyebrows. His post was in as solitary and dismal a place as ever I saw. On either side, a dripping-wet wall of jagged stone, excluding all view but a strip of sky; the perspective one way, only a crooked prolongation of this great dungeon; the shorter perspective in the other direction, terminating in a gloomy red light, and the gloomier entrance to a black tunnel, in whose massive architecture there was a barbarous, depressing, and forbidding air. So little sunlight ever found its way to this spot, that it had an earthy deadly smell; and so much cold wind rushed through it, that it struck chill to me, as if I had left the natural world.

Before he stirred, I was near enough to him to have touched him. Not even then removing his eyes from mine, he stepped back one step, and lifted his hand.

This was a lonesome post to occupy (I said), and it had riveted my attention when I looked down from up yonder. A visitor was a rarity, I should suppose; not an unwelcome rarity, I hoped? In me, he merely saw a man who had been shut up within narrow limits all his life, and who, being at last set free, had a newly-awakened interest in these great works. To such purpose I spoke to him; but I am far from sure of the terms I used, for, besides that I am not happy in opening any conversation, there was something in the man that daunted me.

He directed a most curious look towards the red light near the tunnel's mouth, and looked all about it, as if something were missing from it, and then looked at me.

That light was part of his charge? Was it not?

He answered in a low voice: 'Don't you know it is?'

The monstrous thought came into my mind as I perused the fixed eyes and the saturnine face, that this was a spirit, not a man. I have speculated since, whether there may have been infection in his mind.

In my turn, I stepped back. But in making the action, I detected in his eyes some latent fear of me. This put the monstrous thought to flight.

'You look at me,' I said, forcing a smile, 'as if you had a dread of me.'

'I was doubtful,' he returned, 'whether I had seen you before.'

'Where?'

He pointed to the red light he had looked at.

'There?' I said.

Intently watchful of me, he replied (but without sound), Yes.

'My good fellow, what should I do there? However, be that as it may, I never was there, you may swear.'

'I think I may,' he rejoined. 'Yes. I am sure I may.'

His manner cleared, like my own. He replied to my remarks with readiness, and in well-chosen words. Had he much to do there? Yes; that was to say, he had enough responsibility to bear; but exactness and watchfulness were what was required of him, and of actual work—

manual labour he had next to none. To change that signal, to trim those lights, and to turn this iron handle now and then, was all he had to do under that head. Regarding those many long and lonely hours of which I seemed to make so much, he could only say that the routine of his life had shaped itself into that form, and he had grown used to it. He had taught himself a language down here— if only to know it by sight, and to have formed his own crude ideas of its pronunciation, could be called learning it. He had also worked at fractions and decimals, and tried a little algebra; but he was, and had been as a boy, a poor hand at figures. Was it necessary for him when on duty, always to remain in that channel of damp air, and could he never rise into the sunshine from between those high stone walls? Why, that depended upon times and circumstances. Under some conditions there would be less upon the Line than under others, and the same held good as to certain hours of the day and night. In bright weather, he did choose occasions for getting a little above these lower shadows; but, being at all times liable to be called by his electric bell, and at such times listening for it with redoubled anxiety, the relief was less than I would suppose.

He took me into his box, where there was a fire, a desk for an official book in which he had to make certain entries, a telegraphic instrument with its dial face and needles, and the little bell of which he had spoken. On my trusting that he would excuse the remark that he had been well-educated, and (I hoped I might say without offence), perhaps educated above that station, he observed that instances of slight incongruity in such-wise would rarely be found wanting among large bodies of men; that he had heard it was so in workhouses, in the police force, even in that last desperate resource, the army; and that he knew it was so, more or less, in any great railway staff. He had been, when young (if I could believe it, sitting in that hut; he scarcely could), a student of natural philosophy, and had attended lectures; but he had run wild, misused his opportunities, gone down, and never risen again. He had no complaint to offer about that. He had made his bed, and he lay upon it. It was far too late to make another.

All that I have here condensed, he said in a quiet manner, with his grave dark regards divided between me and the fire. He threw in the word 'Sir' from time to time, and especially when he referred to his youth: as though to request me to understand that he claimed to be nothing but what I found him. He was several times interrupted by the little bell, and had to read off messages, and send replies. Once, he had to stand without the door, and display a flag as a train passed, and make some verbal communication to the driver. In the discharge of his duties I observed him to be remarkably exact and vigilant, breaking off his discourse at a syllable, and remaining silent until what he had to do was done.

In a word, I should have set this man down as one of the safest of men to be employed in that capacity, but for the circumstance that while he was speaking to me he twice broke off with a fallen colour, turned his face towards the little bell when it did *not* ring, opened the door of the hut (which was kept shut to exclude the unhealthy damp), and looked out towards the red light near the mouth of the tunnel. On both of those occasions, he came back to the fire with the inexplicable air upon him which I had remarked, without being able to define, when we were so far asunder.

Said I when I rose to leave him: 'You almost make me think that I have met with a contented man.'

(I am afraid I must acknowledge that I said it to lead him on.)

'I believe I used to be so,' he rejoined, in the low voice in which he had first spoken; 'but I am troubled, sir, I am troubled.'

He would have recalled the words if he could. He had said them, however, and I took them up quickly.

'With what? What is your trouble?'

'It is very difficult to impart, sir. It is very, very difficult to speak of. If ever you make me another visit, I will try to tell you.'

'But I expressly intend to make you another visit. Say, when shall it be?'

'I go off early in the morning, and I shall be on again at ten tomorrow night, sir.'

'I will come at eleven.'

He thanked me, and went out at the door with me. 'I'll show my white light, sir,' he said, in his peculiar low voice, 'till you have found the way up. When you have found it, don't call out! And when you are at the top, don't call out!'

His manner seemed to make the place strike colder to me, but I said no more than 'Very well.'

'And when you come down tomorrow night, don't call out! Let me ask you a parting question. What made you cry "Halloa! Below there!" tonight?'

'Heaven knows,' said I. 'I cried something to that effect —'

'Not to that effect, sir. Those were the very words. I know them well.'

'I admit those were the very words. I said them, no doubt, because I saw you below.'

'For no other reason?'

'What other reason could I possibly have!'

'You had no feeling that they were conveyed to you in any supernatural way?'

'No.'

He wished me good night, and held up his light. I walked by the side of the down Line of rails (with a very disagreeable sensation of a train coming behind me), until I found the path. It was easier to mount than to descend, and I got back to my inn without any adventure.

Punctual to my appointment, I placed my foot on the first notch of the zig-zag next night, as the distant clocks were striking eleven. He was waiting for me at the bottom, with his white light on. 'I have not called out,' I said, when we came close together; 'may I speak now?' 'By all means, sir.' 'Good night then, and here's my hand.' 'Good night sir, and here's mine.' With that, we walked side by side to his box, entered it, closed the door, and sat down by the fire.

'I have made up my mind, sir,' he began, bending forward as soon as we were seated, and speaking in a tone but a little above a whisper, 'that you shall not have to ask me twice what troubles me. I took you for someone else yesterday evening. That troubles me.'

'That mistake?'

'No, that someone else.'

'Who is it?'

'I don't know.'

'Like me?'

'I don't know. I never saw the face. The left arm is across the face, and the right arm is waved. Violently waved. This way.'

I followed his action with my eyes, and it was the action of an arm gesticulating with the utmost passion and vehemence: 'For God's sake clear the way!'

'One moonlight night,' said the man, 'I was sitting here, when I heard a voice cry "Halloa! Below there!" I started up, looked from that door, and saw this Someone else standing by the red light near the tunnel, waving as I just now showed you. The voice seemed hoarse with shouting, and it cried, "Look out! Look out!" And then again "Halloa! Below there! Look out!" I caught up my lamp, turned it on red and ran towards the figure calling, "What's wrong? What has happened? Where?" It stood just outside the blackness of the tunnel. I advanced so close upon it that I wondered at its keeping the sleeve across its eyes. I ran right up at it, and had my hand stretched out to pull the sleeve away, when it was gone.'

'Into the tunnel,' said I.

'No. I ran on into the tunnel, five hundred yards. I stopped and held my lamp above my head, and saw the figures of the measured distance, and saw the wet stains stealing down the walls and trickling through the arch. I ran out again, faster than I had run in (for I had a mortal abhorrence of the place upon me), and I looked all round the red light with my own red light, and I went up the iron ladder to the gallery atop of it, and I came down again, and ran back here. I telegraphed both ways, "An alarm has been given. Is anything wrong?" The answer came back, both ways: "All well."'

Resisting the slow touch of a frozen finger tracing out

my spine, I showed him how that this figure must be a deception of his sense of sight, and how that figures, originating in disease of the delicate nerves that minister to the functions of the eye, were known to have often troubled patients, some of whom had become conscious of the nature of their affliction, and had even proved it by experiments upon themselves. 'As to an imaginary cry,' said I, 'do but listen for a moment to the wind in this unnatural valley while we speak so low, and to the wild harp it makes of the telegraph wires!'

That was all very well, he returned, after we had sat listening for a while, and he ought to know something of the wind and the wires, he who so often passed long winter nights there, alone and watching. But he would beg to remark that he had not finished.

I asked his pardon, and he slowly added these words, touching my arm:

'Within six hours after the Appearance, the memorable accident on this Line happened, and within ten hours the dead and wounded were brought along through the tunnel over the spot where the figure had stood.'

A disagreeable shudder crept over me, but I did my best against it. It was not to be denied, I rejoined, that this was a remarkable coincidence, calculated deeply to impress his mind. But it was unquestionable that remarkable coincidences did continually occur, and they must be taken into account in dealing with such a subject. Though to be sure I must admit, I added (for I thought I saw that he was going to bring the objection to bear upon me), men of common-sense did not allow much for coincidences in making the ordinary calculations of life.

He again begged to remark that he had not finished.

I again begged his pardon for being betrayed into interruptions.

'This,' he said, again laying his hand upon my arm, and glancing over his shoulder with hollow eyes, 'was just a year ago. Six or seven months passed, and I had recovered from the surprise and shock, when one morning, as the day was breaking, I, standing at that door, looked towards the red light, and saw the spectre again.' He stopped, with a fixed look at me.

'Did it cry out?'

'No. It was silent.'

'Did it wave its arm?'

'No. It leaned against the shaft of the light, with both hands before the face. Like this.'

Once more, I followed his action with my eyes. It was an action of mourning. I have seen such attitude in stone figures on tombs.

'Did you go up to it?'

'I came in and sat down, partly to collect my thoughts, partly because it had turned me faint. When I went to the door again, daylight was above me, and the ghost was gone.'

'But nothing followed? Nothing came of this?'

He touched me on the arm with his forefinger twice or thrice, giving a ghastly nod each time.

'That very day, as a train came out of the tunnel, I noticed, at a carriage window on my side, what looked like a confusion of hands and heads, and something waved. I saw it, just in time to signal the driver, Stop! He shut off, and put his brake on, but the train drifted past here a hundred and fifty yards or more. I ran after it, and as I went along, heard terrible screams and cries. A beautiful young lady had died instantaneously in one of the compartments, and was brought in here, and laid down on this floor between us.'

Involuntarily, I pushed my chair back, as I looked from the boards at which he pointed, to himself.

'True, sir. True. Precisely as it happened, so I tell it you.'

I could think of nothing to say, to any purpose, and my mouth was very dry. The wind and the wires took up the story with a long lamenting wail.

He resumed. 'Now, sir, mark this, and judge how my mind is troubled. The spectre came back, a week ago. Ever since, it has been there, now and again, by fits and starts.'

'At the light?'

'At the Danger-light.'

'What does it seem to do?'

He repeated, if possible with increased passion and

23

vehemence, that former gesticulation of 'For God's sake clear the way!'

Then, he went on. 'I have no peace or rest for it. It calls to me, for many minutes together, in an agonised manner, "Below there! Look out! Look out!" It stands waving to me. It rings my little bell —.'

I caught at that. 'Did it ring your bell yesterday evening when I was here, and you went to the door?'

'Twice.'

'Why, see,' said I, 'how your imagination misleads you. My eyes were on the bell, and my ears were open to the bell, and if I am a living man, it did *not* ring at those times. No, nor at any other time, except when it was rung in the natural course of physical things by the station communicating with you.'

He shook his head. 'I have never made a mistake as to that, yet, sir. I have never confused the spectre's ring with the man's. The ghost's ring is a strange vibration in the bell that it derives from nothing else, and I have not asserted that the bell stirs to the eye. I don't wonder that you failed to hear it. But I heard it.'

'And did the spectre seem to be there, when you looked out?'

'It was there.'

'Both times?'

He repeated firmly: 'Both times.'

'Will you come to the door with me, and look for it now?'

He bit his under-lip as though he were somewhat unwilling, but arose. I opened the door, and stood on the step while he stood in the doorway. There, was the Danger-light. There, was the dismal mouth of the tunnel. There, were the high wet stone walls of the cutting. There, were the stars above them.

'Do you see it?' I asked him, taking particular note of his face. His eyes were prominent and strained; but not very much more so, perhaps, than my own had been when I had directed them earnestly towards the same spot.

'No,' he answered. 'It is not there.'

'Agreed,' said I.

We went in again, shut the door, and resumed our seats. I was thinking how best to improve this advantage, if it might be called one, when he took up the conversation in such a matter of course way, so assuming that there could be no serious question of fact between us, that I felt myself placed in the weakest of positions.

'By this time you will fully understand, sir,' he said, 'that what troubles me so dreadfully, is the question, What does the spectre mean?'

I was not sure, I told him, that I did fully understand.

'What is its warning against?' he said, ruminating, with his eyes on the fire, and only by times turning them on me. 'What is the danger? Where is the danger? There is danger overhanging, somewhere on the Line. Some dreadful calamity will happen. It is not to be doubted this third time, after what has gone before. But surely this is a cruel haunting of me. What can I do?'

He pulled out his handkerchief, and wiped the drops from his heated forehead.

'If I telegraph Danger, on either side of me, or on both, I can give no reason for it,' he went on, wiping the palms of his hands. 'I should get into trouble, and do no good. They would think I was mad. This is the way it would work:—Message: "Danger! Take care!" Answer: "What danger? Where?" Message: "Don't know. But for God's sake take care!" They would displace me. What else could they do?'

His pain of mind was most pitiable to see. It was the mental torture of a conscientious man, oppressed beyond endurance by an unintelligible responsibility involving life.

'When it first stood under the Danger-light,' he went on, putting his dark hair back from his head, and drawing his hands outward across and across his temples in an extremity of feverish distress, 'why not tell me where that accident was to happen—if it must happen? Why not tell me how it could be averted—if it could have been averted? When on its second coming it hid its face, why not tell me instead: "She is going to die. Let them keep her at home"? If it came, on those two occasions, only to show me that its warnings were true, and so to prepare me for the third, why not warn me plainly now? And I, Lord help me! A mere poor signalman on this solitary station! Why not go to somebody with credit to be believed and power to act!'

When I saw him in this state, I saw that for the poor man's sake, as well as for the public safety, what I had to do for the time was to compose his mind. Therefore, setting aside all question of reality or unreality between us, I represented to him that whoever thoroughly discharged his duty, must do well, and that at least it was his comfort that he understood his duty, though he did not understand these confounding Appearances. In this effort I succeeded far better than in the attempt to reason him out of his conviction. He became calm; the occupations incidental to his post as the night advanced, began to make larger demands on his attention; and I left him at two in the morning. I had offered to stay through the night, but he would not hear of it.

That I more than once looked at the red light as I ascended the pathway, that I did not like the red light, and that I should have slept but poorly if my bed had been under it, I see no reason to conceal. Nor, did I like the two sequences of the accident and the dead girl. I see no reason to conceal that, either.

But, what ran most in my thoughts was the consideration how ought I to act, having become the recipient of this disclosure? I had proved the man to be intelligent, vigilant, painstaking, and exact; but how long might he remain so, in his state of mind? Though in a subordinate position, still he held a most important trust, and would I (for instance) like to stake my own life on the chances of his continuing to execute it with precision?

Unable to overcome a feeling that there would be something treacherous in my communicating what he had told me, to his superiors in the Company, without first being plain with myself and proposing a middle course to him, I ultimately resolved to offer to accompany him (otherwise keeping his secret for the present) to the wisest medical practitioner we could hear of in those parts, and to take his opinion. A change in his time of duty would come round next night, he had apprised me, and he would be off an hour or two after sunrise, and on again soon after sunset. I had appointed to return accordingly.

Next evening was a lovely evening, and I walked out early to enjoy it. The sun was not yet quite down when I traversed the field-path near the top of the deep cutting. I would extend my walk for an hour, I said to myself, half an hour on and half an hour back, and it would then be time to go to my signalman's box.

Before pursuing my stroll, I stepped to the brink, and mechanically looked down, from the point from which I had first seen him. I cannot describe the thrill that seized upon me, when, close at the mouth of the tunnel, I saw the appearance of a man, with his left sleeve across his eyes, passionately waving his right arm.

The nameless horror that oppressed me, passed in a moment, for in a moment I saw that this appearance of a man was a man indeed, and that there was a little group of other men standing at a short distance, to whom he seemed to be rehearsing the gesture he made. The Danger-light was not yet lighted. Against its shaft, a little low hut, entirely new to me, had been made of some wooden supports and tarpaulin. It looked no bigger than a bed.

With an irresistible sense that something was wrong— with a flashing self-reproachful fear that fatal mischief had come of my leaving the man there, and causing no one to be sent to overlook or correct what he did—I descended the notched path with all the speed I could make.

'What is the matter?' I asked the men.

'Signalman killed this morning, sir.'

'Not the man belonging to that box?'

'Yes, sir.'

'Not the man I know?'

'You will recognise him, sir, if you knew him,' said the man who spoke for the others, solemnly uncovering his own head and raising an end of the tarpaulin, 'for his face is quite composed.'

'O! how did this happen, how did this happen?' I asked, turning from one to another as the hut closed in again.

'He was cut down by an engine, sir. No man in England knew his work better. But somehow he was not clear of the outer rail. It was just at broad day. He had struck the light, and had the lamp in his hand. As the engine came out of the tunnel, his back was towards her, and she cut him down. That man drove her, and was showing how it happened. Show the gentleman, Tom.'

The man, who wore a rough dark dress, stepped back to his former place at the mouth of the tunnel.

'Coming round the curve in the tunnel, sir,' he said, 'I saw him at the end, like as if I saw him down a perspective-glass. There was no time to check speed, and I knew him to be very careful. As he didn't seem to take heed of the whistle, I shut it off when we were running down upon him, and called to him as loud as I could call.'

'What did you say?'

'I said, Below there! Look out! Look out! For God's sake clear the way!'

I started.

'Ah! it was a dreadful time sir. I never left off calling to him. I put this arm before my eyes, not to see, and I waved this arm to the last; but it was no use.'

Without prolonging the narrative to dwell on any one of its curious circumstances more than on any other, I may, in closing it, point out the coincidence that the warning of the engine-driver included, not only the words which the unfortunate signalman had repeated to me as haunting him, but also the words which I myself—not he—had attached, and that only in my own mind, to the gesticulation he had imitated.

THE GARSIDE FELL
DISASTER

L. T. C. Rolt

A tunnel may suggest the mouth of Hell to many of us and, certainly, many, many men have died in the building of Britain's many miles of railway tunnels in conditions reminiscent of Hell itself. No doubt this mental connection suggested the ghost stories that are still told about the Watford Tunnel and the Shrugborough Tunnel (near Rugeley Power Station). Dickens did not see this connection (or chose to disregard it) when he wrote The Signalman for he again used the spectral warning theme, so popular at the time, although the story was set in the very mouth of a tunnel.

On the other hand, L. T. C. Rolt admitted that the following story was inspired by those strange-seeming towers one sees when walking over lonely moors that, from time to time, belch smoke and steam as though they were directly connected with the fires of Hell.

Rolt was a railway enthusiast and an anthologist as well as a writer of macabre stories and had a deep understanding of his subject. Readers of The Garside Fell Disaster will discover a sub-theme of the primitive, the pagan, for the Greek Underworld pre-dated the Christian Hell and the neiblungs and trolls were the first tunnelers.

'YES, I'M AN old railwayman I am, and proud of it. You see, I come of a railway family, as you might say, for I reckon there've been Boothroyds on the railway—in the signal cabin or on the footplate mostly—ever since old Geordie Stephenson was about. We haven't always served the same company. There were four of us. My two elder brothers followed my father on the North-Western, but I joined the Grand Trunk, and Bert, our youngest, he went east to Grantham. He hadn't been long there before he was firing on one of Patrick Stirling's eight-foot singles, the prettiest little locos as ever was or ever will be I reckon. He finished up driver on Ivatt's "Atlantics" while Harry and Fred were working "Jumbos" and "Precursors" out of Crewe. I could have had the footplate job myself easy enough if I'd a mind; took it in with my mother's milk I did, if you follow my meaning. But (and sometimes I'm not sure as I don't regret it) I married early on, and the old woman persuaded me to go for a more settled job, so it was the signal box for me. A driver's wife's a widow most o' the week, unless he happens to click for a regular local turn.

'The first job I had on my own was at Garside on the Carlisle line south of Highbeck Junction, and it was here that this business as I was speaking of happened; a proper bad do it was, and the rummest thing as ever I had happen in all my time.

'Now you could travel the railways from one end to t'other, Scotland and all, but I doubt you'd find a more lonesome spot than Garside, or one so mortal cold in winter. I don't know if you've ever travelled that road, but all I know is it must have cost a mint of money. You see, the Grand Trunk wanted their own road to Scotland, but the East Coast lot had taken the easiest pick, and the North-Western had the next best run through Preston and over Shap, so there was nothing else for them but to carry their road over the mountains. It took a bit of doing, I can tell you, and I know, for when I was up there, there was plenty of folks about who remembered the railway coming. They told me what a game it was what with the snow and the wind, and the clay that was like rock in summer and a treacle pudding in winter.

'Garside Box takes its name from Garside Fell same as the tunnel. There's no station there, for there isn't a house in sight, let alone a village, and my cottage was down at Frithdale about half an hour's walk away. It was what we call a section box, just a small box, the signals, the two "lie-by" roads, one on the up and one on the down side, where goods trains could stand to let the fast trains through if need be. Maybe you know how the block system works; how you can only admit one train on to a section at a time. Well, it would have been an eight-mile section, heavily graded at that, from Highbeck to Ennerthwaite, the next station south, and it might have taken a heavy goods anything up to half an hour to clear it. That's why they made two sections of it by building Garside box just midway between the two. It was over a thousand feet up, not far short of the summit of the line; in fact, looking south from my box I could see that summit, top of the long bank up from Ennerthwaite. Just north of the box was the mouth of the tunnel, a mile and a half of it, under Garside Fell. If ever you should come to walk over those mountains you couldn't miss the ventilation shafts of the tunnel. It looks kind of queer to see those great stone towers a-smoking and steaming away up there in the heather miles and miles from anywhere with not a soul for company and all so quiet. Not that they smoke now as much as they did, but I'll be coming to that presently.

'Well, as I've said before, you could travel the length and breadth of England before you'd find a lonelier place than Garside. Job Micklewright, who was ganger on the section, would generally give me a look up when he went by, and if I switched a goods into the "lie-by", more often than not the fireman or the guard would pass the time of day, give me any news from down the line, and maybe make a can of tea on my stove. But otherwise I wouldn't see a soul from the time I came on till I got my relief. Of course there was the trains, but then you couldn't call them company, not properly speaking. Hundreds and hundreds of folks must have passed me by every day, and yet there I was all on my own with only a few old sheep for company, and the birds crying up on the moor. Funny that, when you come to think of it, isn't it? Mind you, I'm not saying it wasn't grand to be up there on a fine day in summer. You could keep your town life then. It made you feel as it was good to be alive what with the sun a-shining and the heather all out, grasshoppers ticking away and the air fairly humming with bees. Yes, you got to notice little things like that, and as for the smell of that moor in summer, why, I reckon I can smell it now. It was a different tale in winter though. Cold? It fair makes me shiver to think on it. I've known the wind set in the north-east for months on end, what we call a lazy wind—blows through you, see, too tired to go round. Sometimes it blew that strong it was all you could do to stand against it. More than once I had the glass of my windows blown in, and there were times when I thought the whole cabin was going what with the roaring and rattling and shaking of it. Just you imagine climbing a signal ladder to fix a lamp in that sort of weather; it wasn't easy to keep those lamps in, I can tell you. Then there was the snow; you don't know what snow is down here in the south. The company was well off for ploughs and we'd no lack of good engines even in those days, but it used to beat them. Why, I've known it snow for two days and a night, blowing half a gale all the while, and at the end of it there's been a drift of snow twenty feet deep in the cutting up by the tunnel.

'But in spite of all the wind and the snow and the rain (Lord, how it could rain!) it was the mists as I hated most. That may sound funny to you, but then no signalman can a-bear mist and fog, it kind of blinds you, and that makes you uneasy. It's for the signalman to judge whether he shall call out the fogmen, and that's a big responsibility. It may come up sudden after sundown in autumn, you calls your fogmen, and by the time they come on it's all cleared off and they want to know what the hell you're playing at. So another time you put off calling them, but it don't clear, and before you know where you are you've got trains over-running signals. We had no fogmen at Garside, there was little occasion for them, but we kept a box of detonators in the cabin. All the same, I didn't like fog no more for that. They're queer things are those mountain mists. Sometimes all day I'd see one hanging on the moor, perhaps only a hundred yards away, but never seeming to come no nearer. And then all on a sudden down it would come so thick that in a minute, no more, I couldn't see my home signals. But there was another sort of fog at Garside that I liked even less, and that was the sort that came out from the tunnel. Ah, now that strikes you as funny, doesn't it? Maybe you're thinking that with such a lonesome job I took to fancying things. Oh, I know, I know, if you're a nervy chap it's easy to see things in the mist as have no right to be there, or to hear queer noises when really it's only the wind shouting around or humming in the wires. But I wasn't that sort, and what's more I wasn't the only one who found out that there was something as wasn't quite right about Garside. No, you can take it from me that what I'm telling you is gospel, as true as I'm sitting in this bar a-talking to you.

'No doubt you've often looked at the mouth of a railway tunnel and noticed how the smoke comes a-curling out even though there may be not a sight or sound of any traffic. Well, the first thing I noticed about Garside tunnel was that, for all its ventilation shafts, it was the smokiest hole I'd ever seen. Not that this struck me as queer, at least not at first. I remember, though, soon after I came there I was walking up from Frithdale one Monday morning for the early turn and saw that number two shaft way up on the fell was smoking like a factory chimney. That did seem a bit strange, for there was precious little traffic through on a Sunday in those days; in fact, Garside box was locked out and they worked the full eight-mile section. Still, I didn't give much thought to it until one night about three weeks later. It was almost dark, but not so dark that I couldn't just see the tunnel mouth and the whitish-looking smoke sort of oozing out of it. Now, both sections were clear, mind; the last train through had been an up Class A goods and I'd had the "out of section" from Highbeck south box a good half-hour before. But, believe it or not, that smoke grew more and more as I watched it. At first I thought it must be a trick of the wind blowing through the tunnel, though the air seemed still enough for once in a way. But it went on coming out thicker and thicker until I couldn't see the tunnel itself at all, and it came up the cutting toward my box for all the world like a wall of fog. One minute there was a clear sky overhead, the next minute—gone—and the smell of it was fit to choke you. Railway tunnels are smelly holes at the best of times, but that smell was different somehow, and worse than anything I've ever struck. It was so thick round my box that I was thinking of looking out my fog signals, when a bit of a breeze must have got up, for all on a sudden it was gone as quick as it came. The moon was up, and there was the old tunnel plain in the moonlight, just smoking away innocent like as though nothing had happened. Fair made me rub my eyes. "Alf," I said to myself, "you've been dreaming" but all the while I knew I hadn't.

"At first I thought I'd best keep it to myself, but the same thing happened two or three times in the next month or so until one day, casual like, I mentioned it to Perce Shaw who was my relief. He'd had it happen, too, it seemed, but like me he hadn't felt like mentioning it to anyone. "Well," I says to him, "it's my opinion there's something queer going on, something that's neither right nor natural. But if there's one man who should know more than what we do it's Job Micklewright. After all," I says, "he walks through the blinking tunnel."

'Job didn't need much prompting to start him off. The very next morning it was, if I remember rightly. The old tunnel was smoking away as usual when out he comes.

He climbs straight up into my box, blows out his light, and sits down by my stove a-warming himself, for the weather was sharp. "Cold morning," I says. "Ah," he says, rubbing his hands. "Strikes cold, it does, after being in there." "Why?" I asks. "Is it that warm inside there then, Job? It certainly looks pretty thick. Reckon you must have a job to see your way along." Job said nothing for a while, only looked at me a bit old-fashioned, and went on rubbing his hands. Then he says, quiet like, "I reckon you won't be seeing much more of me, Alf." That surprised me. "Why?" I asks. "Because I've put in for a shift," he says. "I've had enough of this beat." "How's that, Job?" I says. "Don't you fancy that old tunnel?" He looked up sharp at that. "What makes you talk that road?" he asks. "Have you noticed something, too, then?" I nodded my head, and told him what I'd seen, which was little enough really when you come to weigh it up. But Job went all serious over it. "Alf," he says, "I've been a good chapel man all my life, I never touch a drop of liquor, you know that, and you know as I wouldn't tell you the word of a lie. Well, then, I'm telling you, Alf," he says, "as that tunnel's no fit place for a God-fearing man. What you've seen's the least of it. I know no more than you what it may be, but there's something in there that I don't want no more truck with, something I fear worse than the day of judgment. It's bad, and its getting worse. That's why I'm going to flit. At first I noticed nothing funny except it was a bit on the smoky side and never seemed to clear proper. Then I found it got terrible stuffy and hot in there, especially between two and three shafts. Very dry it is in there, not a wet patch anywhere, and one day when I dodged into a manhole to let a train by, I found the bricks was warm. "That's a rum do," I says to myself. Since then the smoke or the fog or whatever it may be has been getting thicker, and maybe it's my fancy or maybe it's not, but it strikes me that there's queer things moving about in it, things I couldn't lay name to even if I could see them proper. And as for the heat, it's proper stifling. Why I could take you in now and you'd find as you couldn't bear your hand on the bricks round about the place I know of. This last couple or three days it has been the worst of all, for I've seen lights a-moving and darting about in the smoke, mostly round about the shaft openings, only little ones mind, but kind of flickering like flames, only they don't make no sound, and the heat in there fit to smother you. I've kept it to myself till now, haven't even told the missus, for I thought if I let on, folks would think I was off my head. What it all means, Alf, only the Lord himself knows, all I know is I've had enough."

'Now I must say, in spite of what I'd seen, I took old Job's yarn with a pinch of salt myself until a couple of nights after, and then I saw something that made me feel that maybe he was right after all. It had just gone dark, and I was walking back home down to Frithdale, when, chancing to look round, I saw there was a light up on the Fell. It was just a kind of a dull glow shining on smoke, like as if the moor was afire somewhere just out of sight over the ridge. But it wasn't the time of year for heather burning—the moor was like a wet sponge—and when I looked again I saw without much doubt that it was coming from the tunnel shafts. Mind you, I wouldn't have cared to stake my oath on it at the time. It was only faint, like, but I didn't like the look of it at all.

'That was the night of February the first, 1897, I can tell you that because it was exactly a fortnight to the night of the Garside disaster, and that's a date I shall never forget as long as I live. I can remember it all as though it were yesterday. It was a terrible rough night, raining heavens hard, and the wind that strong over the moor you could hardly stand against it. I was on the early turn that week, so the missus and I had gone to bed about ten. The next thing I knew was her a-shaking and shaking at my shoulder and calling, "Alf, Alf, wake up, there's summat up." What with the wind roaring and rattling round, it was a job to hear yourself think. "What's up?" I asks, fuddled like. "Look out of the window," she cries out, "there's a fire up on the Fell; summat's up I tell you." Next minute I was pulling on my clothes, for there wasn't any doubt about it this time. Out there in the dark the tunnel shafts were flaming away like ruddy beacons. Just you try to imagine a couple of those old-fashioned iron furnaces flaring out on the top of a mountain at the back of beyond, and you'll maybe understand why the sight put the fear of God into us.

'I set off up to Garside Box just as fast as I could go, and most of the menfolk out of the village after me, for many of them had been wakened by the noise of the storm, and those who hadn't soon got the word. I had a hurricane-lamp with me, but I could hardly see the box for the smoke that was blowing down the cutting from the tunnel. Inside I found Perce Shaw in a terrible taking. His hair was all singed, his face was as white as that wall, and "My God", or "You can't do nothing", was all he'd say, over and over again. I got through to Ennerthwaite and Highbeck South and found that they'd already had the "obstruction danger" from Perce. Then I set detonators on the down line, just in case, and went off up to the tunnel. But I couldn't do no good. What with the heat and the smoke I was suffocating before I'd got a hundred yards inside. By the time I'd got back to the box I found that Job Micklewright and some of the others had come up, and that they'd managed to quiet Perce enough to tell us what had happened.

'At half-past midnight, it seems, he took an up goods from Highbeck South Box and a few minutes later got the "entering section". Ten minutes after that he accepted the down night "Mountaineer" from Ennerthwaite. (That was one of our crack trains in those days—night sleeper with mails, first stop Carlisle.) Now it's a bank of one in seventy most of the way up from Highbeck, so it might take a heavy goods quarter of an hour to clear the section, but when the fifteen minutes was up and still no sign of her, Perce began to wonder a bit—thought she must be steaming bad. Then he caught the sound of the "Mountaineer" beating it up the bank from Ennerthwaite well up to her time, for the wind was set that road, but he didn't see no cause then to hold her up, Highbeck having accepted her. But just as he heard her top the bank and start gathering speed, a great column of smoke came driving down the cutting and he knew that there was something wrong, for there was no question of it being anything but smoke this time. Whatever was up in the tunnel it was too late to hold up the "Mountaineer"; he put his home "on", but she'd already passed the distant and he doubted whether her driver saw it in the smoke. The smoke must have warned him, though, for he thought he heard him shut off and put on the vacuum just as he went into the tunnel. But he was travelling very fast, and he must have been too late. He hoped that the noise he heard, distant like, was only the wind, but running as she was she should have cleared Highbeck South Box in under four minutes, so when the time went by and no "out of section" came through (what he must've felt waiting there for that little bell to ring twice and once) he sent out the "obstruction danger", both roads, and went off up the line to see what he could do.

"What exactly happened in that tunnel we never shall know. We couldn't get in for twenty-four hours on account of the heat, and then we found both trains burnt out, and not a mortal soul alive. At the inquiry they reckoned a spark from the goods loco must have set her train afire while she was pulling up the bank through the tunnel. The engine of the "Mountaineer" was de-railed. They thought her driver, seeing he couldn't pull up his train in time, had taken the only chance and put on speed hoping to get his train by, but that burning wreckage had fouled his road. Perce got no blame, but then we only told them what we *knew* and not what we *thought*. Perce and I and especially Job Micklewright might have said a lot more than we did, but it wouldn't have done no good, and it might have done us a lot of harm. The three of us got moved from Garside after that—mighty glad we were to go, too—I've never heard anything queer about the place since.

'Mind you, we talked about it a lot between ourselves. Perce and I reckoned the whole thing was a sort of warning of what was going to happen. But Job, who was a local chap born and bred, he thought different. He said that way back in the old days they had another name for Garside Fell. Holy Mountain they called it, though to my way of thinking "unholy" would have been nearer the mark. When he was a little 'un, it seems the old folks down in Frithdale and round about used to tell queer tales about it. Anyway, Job had some funny idea in his head that there was something in that old mountain that should never have been disturbed, and he reckoned the fire kind of put things right again. Sort of a sacrifice, if you follow my meaning. I can't say I hold with such notions myself, but that's my tale of what the papers called the Garside Fell Disaster, and you can make of it what you like.'

THE ENGINEER

Amelia B. Edwards

It was the 'second generation' of railway engineers, men who had assisted the Stephensons, Brunel and Locke, who expanded the building of railways from Britain into Europe. Men such as Thomas Jackson Woodhouse and Thomas Brassey constructed railways in France from as early as 1840, overcoming more difficult civil engineering problems than had presented themselves in Britain because of the more difficult terrain. Owing to the superiority of British workmen over the local inhabitants, Brassey shipped 5,000 men to France in 1841 to work on the Paris and Rouen Railway. At first even the tools, rails and other iron-work had to be shipped from England because France had no industry to supply them; and so the railway explosion began.

Woodhouse went to France in 1843 to build a canal, but the spell of the steam-engine overtook him and he joined Brassey on building the Orleans, Tours and Bordeaux Railway. All this came to an end at the outbreak of the French Revolution in 1848 and the engineers moved on to Spain and then Italy where a great deal of work was waiting to be done. Both Brassey and Woodhouse were building the Turin and Novara Railway when the latter died. It is said that the turn-out for the funeral of this much-respected man was the largest ever seen in Turin for the funeral of a protestant but, no doubt, a great number of his countrymen were present.

At the same time women were at the forefront as writers of macabre stories. In particular, two were admired by Dickens, Mrs Elizabeth Gaskell (who died in 1865) and Amelia B. Edwards. Besides being able to imbue their stories with terror, they had a special ability to contrast good and evil, which many later writers were to copy. In The Engineer Amelia Edwards turns her pen to the subject of the engineer and his work in Europe and treated it in the way for which she was justly famous.

His NAME, SIR, was Matthew Price; mine is Benjamin Hardy. We were born within a few days of each other; bred up in the same village; taught at the same school. I cannot remember the time when we were not close friends. Even as boys, we never knew what it was to quarrel. We had not a thought, we had not a possession, that was not in common. We would have stood by each other, fearlessly, to the death. It was such a friendship as one reads about sometimes in books: fast and firm as the great Tors upon our native moorlands, true as the sun in the heavens.

The name of our village was Chadleigh. Lifted high above the pasture flats which stretched away at our feet like a measureless green lake and melted into mist on the furthest horizon, it nestled, a tiny stone-built hamlet, in a sheltered hollow about midway between the plain and the plateau. Above us, rising ridge beyond ridge, slope beyond slope, spread the mountainous moor-country, bare and bleak for the most part, with here and there a patch of cultivated field or hardy plantation, and crowned highest of all with masses of huge grey crag, abrupt, isolated, hoary, and older than the deluge. These were the Tors—Druids' Tor, King's Tor, Castle Tor, and the like; sacred places, as I have heard, in the ancient time, where crownings, burnings, human sacrifices, and all kinds of bloody heathen rites were performed. Bones, too, have been found there, and arrow-heads, and ornaments of gold and glass. I had a vague awe of the Tors in those boyish days, and would not have gone near them after dark for the heaviest bribe.

I have said that we were born in the same village. He was the son of a small farmer, named William Price, and the eldest of a family of seven; I was the only child of Ephraim Hardy, the Chadleigh blacksmith—a well-known man in those parts, whose memory is not forgotten to this day. Just so far as a farmer is supposed to be a bigger man than a blacksmith, Mat's father might be said to have a better standing than mine; but William Price with his small holding and his seven boys, was, in fact, as poor as many a day-labourer; whilst, the blacksmith, well-to-do, bustling, popular, and open-handed, was a person of some importance in the place.

All this, however, had nothing to do with Mat and myself. It never occurred to either of us that his jacket was out at elbows, or that our mutual funds came altogether from my pocket. It was enough for us that we sat on the same school-bench, conned our tasks from the same primer, fought each other's battles, screened each other's faults, fished, nutted, played truant, robbed orchards and birds' nests together, and spent every half-hour, authorised or stolen, in each others' society. It was a happy time; but it could not go on for ever. My father, being prosperous, resolved to put me forward in the world. I must know more, and do better, than himself. The forge was not good enough, the little world of Chadleigh not wide enough, for me. Thus it happened that I was still swinging the satchel when Mat was whistling at the plough, and that at last, when my future course was shaped out, we were separated, as it then seemed to us, for life. For, blacksmith's son as I was, furnace and forge, in some form or other, pleased me best, and I chose to be a working engineer. So my father by-and-by apprenticed me to a Birmingham iron-master; and, having bidden farewell to Mat, and Chadleigh, and the grey old Tors in the shadow of which I had spent all the days of my life, I turned my face northward, and went over into 'the Black Country'.

I am not going to dwell on this part of my story. How I worked out the term of my apprenticeship; how, when I had served my full time and become a skilled workman, I took Mat from the plough and brought him over to the

Black Country, sharing with him lodging, wages, experience—all, in short, that I had to give; how he, naturally quick to learn and brimful of quiet energy, worked his way up a step at a time, and came by-and-by to be a 'first hand' in his own department; how, during all these years of change, and trial, and effort, the old boyish affection never wavered or weakened, but went on, growing with our growth and strengthening with our strength—are facts which I need do no more than outline in this place.

About this time—it will be remembered that I speak of the days when Mat and I were on the bright side of thirty—it happened that our firm contracted to supply six first-class locomotives to run on the new line, then in process of construction, between Turin and Genoa. It was the first Italian order we had taken. We had had dealings with France, Holland, Belgium, Germany; but never with Italy. The connection, therefore, was new and valuable—all the more valuable because our Transalpine neighbours had but lately begun to lay down the iron roads, and would be safe to need more of our good English work as they went on. So the Birmingham firm set themselves to the contract with a will, lengthened our working hours, increased our wages, took on fresh hands, and determined, if energy and promptitude could do it, to place themselves at the head of the Italian labour-market, and stay there. They deserved and achieved success. The six locomotives were not only turned out to time, but were shipped, dispatched and delivered with a promptitude that fairly amazed our Piedmontese consignee. I was not a little proud, you may be sure, when I found myself appointed to superintend the transport of the engines. Being allowed a couple of assistants, I contrived that Mat should be one of them; and thus we enjoyed together the first great holiday of our lives.

It was a wonderful change for two Birmingham operatives fresh from the Black Country. The fairy city, with its crescent background of Alps; the port crowded with strange shipping; the marvellous blue sky and the bluer sea; the painted houses on the quays; the quaint cathedral, faced with black and white marble; the street of jewellers, like an Arabian Nights' bazaar; the street of palaces, with its Moorish courtyards, its fountains and orange trees; the women veiled like brides; the galley-slaves chained two and two; the processions of priests and friars; the everlasting clangour of bells; the babble of a strange tongue; the singular lightness and brightness of the climate—made, altogether such a combination of wonders that we wandered about, the first day, in a kind of bewildered dream, like children at a fair. Before that week was ended, being tempted by the beauty of the place and the liberality of the pay, we had agreed to take service with the Turin and Genoa Railway Company, and to turn our backs upon Birmingham for ever.

Then began a new life—a life so active and healthy, so steeped in fresh air and sunshine, that we sometimes marvelled how we could have endured the gloom of the Black Country. We were constantly up and down the line; now at Genoa, now at Turin, taking trial trips with the locomotives, and placing our old experiences at the service of our new employers.

In the meanwhile we made Genoa our headquarters, and hired a couple of rooms over a small shop in a by-street sloping down to the quays. Such a busy little street—so steep and winding that no vehicles could pass through it, and so narrow that the sky looked like a mere strip of deep blue ribbon overhead! Every house in it, however, was a shop, where the goods encroached on the footway, or were piled about the door, or hung like tapestry from the balconies; and all day long, from dawn to dusk, an incessant stream of passers-by poured up and down between the port and the upper quarter of the city.

Our landlady was the widow of a silver-worker, and lived by the sale of filigree ornaments, cheap jewellery, combs, fans and toys in ivory and jet. She had an only daughter named Gianetta, who served in the shop, and was simply the most beautiful woman I ever beheld. Looking back across this weary chasm of years, and bringing her image before me (as I can and do) with all the vividness of life, I am unable, even now, to detect a flaw in her beauty. I do not attempt to describe her. I do not believe there is a poet living who could find the words to do it; but I once saw a picture that was somewhat like her (not half so lovely, but still like her), and, for aught I know, that picture is still hanging where I last looked at it—upon the walls of the Louvre. It represented a woman with brown eyes and golden hair, looking over her shoulder into a circular mirror held by a bearded man in the background. In this man, as I then understood, the artist had painted his own portrait; in her, the portrait of the woman he loved. No picture that I ever saw was half so beautiful, and yet it was not worthy to be named in the same breath with Gianetta Coneglia.

You may be certain the widow's shop did not want for customers. All Genoa knew how fair a face was to be seen behind that dingy little counter; and Gianetta, flirt as she was, had more lovers than she cared to remember, even by name. Gentle and simple, rich and poor, from the red-capped sailor buying his ear-rings or his amulet, to the nobleman carelessly purchasing half the filigrees in the window, she treated them all alike—encouraged them, laughed at them, led them on and turned them off at her pleasure. She had no more heart than a marble statue; as Mat and I discovered by-and-by, to our bitter cost.

I cannot tell to this day how it came about, or what first led me to suspect how things were going with us both; but long before the waning of that autumn a coldness had sprung up between my friend and myself. It was nothing that could have been put into words. It was nothing that either of us could have explained or justified, to save his life. We lodged together, ate together, worked together, exactly as before; we even took our long evening's walk together, when the day's labour was ended; and except, perhaps, that we were more silent than of old, no mere looker-on could have detected a shadow of change. Yet there it was, silent and subtle, widening the gulf between us every day.

It was not his fault. He was too true and gentle-hearted to have willingly brought about such a state of things between us. Neither do I believe—fiery as my nature is—that it was mine. It was all hers—hers from first to last—

the sin, and the shame, and the sorrow.

If she had shown a fair and open preference for either of us, no real harm could have come of it. I would have put any constraint upon myself, and, Heaven knows! have borne any suffering, to see Mat really happy. I know that he would have done the same, and more if he could, for me. But Gianetta cared not one sou for either. She never meant to choose between us. It gratified her vanity to divide us; it amused her to play with us. It would pass my power to tell how, by a thousand imperceptible shades of coquetry—by the lingering of a glance, the substitution of a word, the flitting of a smile—she contrived to turn our heads, and torture our hearts, and lead us on to love her. She deceived us both. She buoyed us both up with hope; she maddened us with jealousy; she crushed us with despair. For my part, when I seemed to wake to a sudden sense of the ruin that was about our path and I saw how the truest friendship that ever bound two lives together was drifting on to wreck and ruin, I asked myself whether any woman in the world was worth what Mat had been to me and I to him. But this was not often. I was readier to shut my eyes upon the truth than to face it; and so lived on; wilfully, in a dream.

Thus the autumn passed away, and winter came—the strange treacherous Genoese winter, green with olive and ilex, brilliant with sunshine, and bitter with storm. Still, rivals at heart and friends on the surface, Mat and I lingered on in our lodgings in the Vicolo Balba. Still Gianetta held us with her fatal wiles and her still more fatal beauty. At length there came a day when I felt I could bear the horrible misery and suspense of it no longer. The sun, I vowed, should not go down before I knew my sentence. She must choose between us. She must either take me or let me go. I was reckless. I was desperate. I was determined to know the worst, or the best. If the worst, I would at once turn by back upon Genoa, upon her, upon all the pursuits and purposes of my past life, and begin the world anew. This I told her, passionately and sternly, standing before her in the little parlour at the back of the shop, one bleak December morning.

'If it's Mat whom you care for most,' I said, 'tell me so in one word, and I will never trouble you again. He is better worth your love. I am jealous and exacting; he is as trusting and unselfish as a woman. Speak, Gianetta; am I to bid you good-bye for ever and ever, or am I to write home to my mother in England, bidding her pray to God to bless the woman who has promised to be my wife?'

'You plead your friend's cause well,' she replied, haughtily. 'Matteo ought to be grateful. This is more than he ever did for you.'

'Give me my answer, for pity's sake,' I exclaimed, 'and let me go!'

'You are free to go or stay, Signor Inglese,' she replied. 'I am not your jailor.'

'Do you bid me leave you?'

'Beata Madre! Not I.'

'Will you marry me, if I stay?'

She laughed aloud—such a merry, mocking, musical laugh, like a chime of silver bells!

'You ask too much,' she said.

'Only what you have led me to hope these five or six months past!'

'That is just what Matteo says. How tiresome you both are!'

'O, Gianetta,' I said passionately, 'be serious for one moment! I am a rough fellow, it is true—not half good enough or clever enough for you; but I love you with my whole heart, and an Emperor could do no more.'

'I am glad of it,' she replied, 'I do not want you to love me less.'

'Then you cannot wish to make me wretched! Will you promise me?'

'I promise nothing,' said she, with another burst of laughter; 'except that I will not marry Matteo!'

Except that she would not marry Matteo! Only that. Not a word of hope for myself. Nothing but my friend's condemnation. I might get comfort, and selfish triumph, and some sort of base assurance out of that, if I could. And so, to my shame, I did. I grasped at the vain encouragement, and, fool that I was, let her put me off again unanswered. From that day, I gave up all effort at self-control, and let myself drift blindly on—to destruction.

At length things became so bad between Mat and myself that it seemed as if an open rupture must be at hand. We avoided each other, scarcely exchanged a dozen sentences in a day, and fell away from all our old familiar habits. At this time—I shudder to remember it—there were moments when I felt that I hated him.

Thus, with the trouble deepening and widening between us day by day, another month or five weeks went by; and February came; and, with February, the Carnival. They said in Genoa that it was a particularly dull carnival; and so it must have been; for, save a flag or two hung out in some of the principal streets, and a sort of fiesta look about the women, there were no special indications of the season. It was, I think, the second day when, having been on the line all the morning, I returned to Genoa at dusk, and, to my surprise, found Mat Price on the platform. He came up to me, and laid his hand on my arm.

'You are in late,' he said, 'I have been waiting for you three-quarters of an hour. Shall we dine together today?'

Impulsive as I am, this evidence of returning goodwill at once called up my better feelings.

'With all my heart, Mat,' I replied, 'shall we go to Gozzoli's?'

'No, no,' he said, hurriedly. 'Some quieter place—some place where we can talk. I have something to say to you.'

I noticed now that he looked pale and agitated, and an uneasy sense of apprehension stole upon me. We decided on the 'Pescatore,' a little out-of-the-way trattoria, down near the Malo Vecchio. There, in a dingy salon, frequented chiefly by seamen, and redolent of tobacco, we ordered our simple dinner. Mat scarcely swallowed a morsel; but, calling presently for a bottle of Sicilian wine, drank eagerly.

'Well, Mat,' I said, as the last dish was placed on the table, 'what news have you?'

'Bad.'

'I guessed that from your face.'

'Bad for you—bad for me. Gianetta.'

'What of Gianetta?'

He passed his hand nervously across his lips.

'Gianetta is false—worse than false,' he said, in a hoarse voice. 'She values an honest man's heart just as she values a flower for her hair—wears it for a day, then throws it aside for ever. She has cruelly wronged us both.'

'In what way? Good Heavens, speak out!'

'In the worst way that a woman can wrong those who love her. She has sold herself to the Marchese Loredano.'

The blood rushed to my head and face in a burning torrent. I could scarcely see, and dared not trust myself to speak.

'I saw her going towards the cathedral,' he went on, hurriedly. 'It was about three hours ago. I thought she might be going to confession, so I hung back and followed her at a distance. When she got inside, however, she went straight to the back of the pulpit, where this man was waiting for her. You remember him—an old man who used to haunt the shop a month or two back. Well, seeing how deep in conversation they were, and how they stood close under the pulpit with their backs towards the church, I fell into a passion of anger and went straight up the aisle, intending to say or do something; I scarcely knew what; but at all events, to draw her arm through mine, and take her home. When I came within a few feet, however, and found only a big pillar between myself and them, I paused. They could not see me, nor I them; but I could hear their voices distinctly, and—I listened.'

'Well, and you heard—.'

'The terms of a shameful bargain—beauty on the one side, gold on the other; so many thousand francs a year; a villa near Naples—Pah! it makes me sick to repeat it.'

And, with a shudder, he poured out another glass of wine and drank it at a draught.

'After that,' he said, presently, 'I made no effort to bring her away. The whole thing was so cold-blooded, so deliberate, so shameful, that I felt I had only to wipe her out of my memory, and leave her to her fate. I stole out of the cathedral, and walked about here by the sea for ever so long, trying to get my thoughts straight. Then I remembered you, Ben; and the recollection of how this wanton had come between us and broken up our lives drove me wild. So I went up to the station and waited for you. I felt you ought to know it all; and I thought, perhaps, that we might go back to England together.'

'The Marchese Loredano!'

It was all that I could say; all that I could think. As Mat had just said of himself, I felt 'like one stunned'.

'There is one other thing I may as well tell you,' he added, reluctantly, 'if only to show you how false a woman can be. We—we were to have been married next month.'

'We? Who? What do you mean?'

'I mean that we were to have been married—Gianetta and I.'

A sudden storm of rage, of scorn, of incredulity, swept over me at this, and seemed to carry my senses away.

'You!' I cried out. 'Gianetta marry you! I don't believe it.'

'I wish I had not believed it,' he replied, looking up as if puzzled by my vehemence. 'But she promised me; and I thought, when she promised it, she meant it.'

'She told me, weeks ago, that she would never be your wife!'

His colour rose, his brow darkened; but when his answer came, it was as calm as the last.

'Indeed!' he said. 'Then it is only one baseness more. She told me that she had refused you; and that was why we kept our engagement secret.'

'Tell the truth, Mat Price,' I said, well-nigh beside myself with suspicion. 'Confess that every word of this is false! Confess that Gianetta will not listen to you, and that you are afraid I may succeed where you have failed. As perhaps I shall—as perhaps I shall, after all!'

'Are you mad?' he exlaimed. 'What do you mean?'

'That I believe it's just a trick to get me away to England—that I don't credit a syllable of your story. You're a liar, and I hate you!'

He rose, and, lying one hand on the back of his chair, looked me sternly in the face.

'If you were not Benjamin Hardy,' he said, deliberately, 'I would thrash you within an inch of your life.'

'The words had no sooner passed his lips than I sprang at him. I have never been able distinctly to remember what followed. A curse—a blow—a struggle—a moment of blind fury—a cry—a confusion of tongues—a circle of strange faces. Then I see Mat lying back in the arms of a bystander; myself trembling and bewildered—the knife dropping from my grasp; blood upon the floor; blood upon my hands; blood upon his shirt. And then I hear those dreadful words:

'O, Ben, you have murdered me!'

He did not die—at least, not there and then. He was carried to the nearest hospital, and lay for some weeks between life and death. His case, they said, was difficult and dangerous. The knife had gone in just below the collar-bone, and pierced down into the lungs. He was not allowed to speak or turn—scarcely to breathe with freedom. He might not even lift his head to drink. I sat by him day and night all through that sorrowful time. I gave up my situation on the railway; I quitted my lodging in the Vicolo Balba; I tried to forget that such a woman as Gianetta Coneglia had ever drawn breath. I lived only for Mat; and he tried to live more, I believe, for my sake than his own. Thus, in the bitter silent hours of pain and penitence, when no hand but mine approached his lips or smoothed his pillow, the old friendship came back with even more than its old trust and faithfulness. He forgave me, fully and freely; and I would thankfully have given my life for him.

At length there came one bright spring morning, when, dismissed as convalescent, he tottered out through the hospital gates, leaning on my arm, and feeble as an infant. He was not cured; neither, as I then learned to my horror and anguish, was it possible that he ever could be cured. He might live, with care, for some years; but the lungs were injured beyond hope of remedy, and a strong or healthy man he could never be again. These, spoken aside to me, were the parting words of the chief physician, who advised me to take him further south without delay.

I took him to a little coast-town called Rocca, some thirty miles beyond Genoa—a sheltered lonely place along the Riviera, where the sea was even bluer than the sky, and the cliffs were green with strange tropical plants, cacti, and aloes, and Egyptian palms. Here we lodged in the house of a small tradesman; and Mat, to use his own words, 'set to work at getting well in good earnest'. But, alas! it was a work which no earnestness could forward. Day after day he went down to the beach, and sat for hours drinking the sea air and watching the sails that came and went in the offing.

By-and-by he could go no further than the garden of the house in which we lived. A little later, and he spent his days on a couch beside the open window, waiting patiently for the end. Ay, for the end! It had come to that. He was fading fast, waning with the waning summer, and conscious that the Reaper was at hand. His whole aim now was to soften the agony of my remorse, and prepare me for what must shortly come.

'I would not live longer, if I could,' he said, lying on his couch one summer evening, and looking up to the stars. 'If I had my choice at this moment, I would ask to go. I should like Gianetta to know that I forgave her.'

'She shall know it,' I said, trembling suddenly from head to foot.

He pressed my hand.

'And you'll write to father?'

'I will.'

I had drawn a little back, that he might not see the tears raining down my cheeks; but he raised himself on his elbow, and looked round.

'Don't fret, Ben,' he whispered; laid his head back wearily upon the pillow—and so died.

And this was the end of it. This was the end of all that made life life to me. I buried him there, in hearing of the wash of a strange sea on a strange shore. I stayed by the grave till the priest and the bystanders were gone. I saw the earth filled in to the last sod, and the gravedigger stamped it down with his feet. Then, and not till then, I felt that I had lost him for ever—the friend I had loved, and hated, and slain. Then, and not till then, I knew that all rest, and joy, and hope were over for me. From that moment my heart hardened within me, and my life was filled with loathing. Day and night, land and sea, labour and rest, food and sleep, were alike hateful to me. It was the curse of Cain, and that my brother had pardoned me made it lie none the lighter. Peace on earth was for me no more, and goodwill towards men was dead in my heart for ever. Remorse softens some natures; but it poisoned mine. I hated all mankind; but above all mankind I hated the woman who had come between us two, and ruined both our lives.

He had bidden me seek her out, and be the messenger of his forgiveness. I had sooner have gone down to the port of Genoa and taken upon me the serge cap and shotted chain of any galley-slave at his toil in the public works; but for all that I did my best to obey him. I went back, alone and on foot. I went back, intending to say to her, 'Gianetta Coneglia, he forgave you; but God never will.' But she was gone. The little shop was let to a fresh occupant; and the neighbours only knew that mother and daughter had left the place quite suddenly, and that Gianetta was supposed to be under the 'protection' of the Marchese Loredano. How I made inquiries here and there—how I heard that they had gone to Naples—and how, being restless and reckless of my time, I worked my passage in a French steamer, and followed her—how, having found the sumptuous villa that was now hers, I learned that she had left there some ten days and gone to Paris, where the Marchese was ambassador for the Two Sicilies—how, working my passage back again to Marseilles, and thence, in part by the river and in part by the rail, I made my way to Paris—how, day after day, I paced the streets and the parks, watched at the ambassador's gates, followed his carriage, and at last, after weeks of waiting, discovered her address—how, having written to request an interview, her servants spurned me from her door and flung my letter in my face—how, looking up at her windows, I then, instead of forgiving, solemnly cursed her with the bitterest curses my tongue could devise—and how, this done, I shook the dust of Paris from my feet, and became a wanderer upon the face of the earth, are facts which I have now no space to tell.

The next six or eight years of my life were shifting and unsettled enough. A morose and restless man, I took employment here and there, as opportunity offered, turning my hand to many things, and caring little what I earned, so long as the work was hard and the change incessant. First of all I engaged myself as chief engineer in one of the French steamers plying between Marseilles and Constantinople. At Constantinople I changed to one of the Austrian Lloyd's boats, and worked for some time to and from Alexandria, Jaffa, and those parts. After that, I fell in with a party of Mr Layard's men at Cairo, and so went up the Nile and took a turn at the excavations of the mound of Nimroud.

Then I became a working engineer on the new desert line between Alexandria and Suez; and by-and-by I worked my passage out to Bombay, and took service as an engine fitter on one of the great Indian railways. I stayed a long time in India; that is to say, I stayed nearly two years, which was a long time for me; and I might not even have left so soon, but for the war that was declared just then with Russia. That tempted me. For I loved danger and hardship as other men love safety and ease; and as for my life, I had sooner have parted from it than kept it, any day. So I came straight back to England; betook myself to Portsmouth, where my testimonials at once procured me the sort of berth I wanted. I went out to the Crimea in the engine-room of one of her Majesty's war steamers.

I served with the fleet, of course, while the war lasted; and when it was over, went wandering off again, rejoicing in my liberty. This time I went to Canada, and after working on a railway then in progress near the American frontier, I presently passed over into the States; journeyed from north to south; crossed the Rocky Mountains; tried a month or two of life in the gold country; and then, being seized with a sudden, aching, unaccountable longing to revisit that solitary grave so far away on the Italian coast, I turned my face once more towards Europe.

Poor little grave! I found it rank with weeds, the cross half shattered, the inscription half effaced. It was as if no one had loved him, or remembered him. I went back to the house in which we had lodged together. The same people were still living there, and made me kindly welcome. I stayed with them for some weeks. I weeded, and planted, and trimmed the grave with my own hands, and set up a fresh cross in pure white marble. It was the first season of rest that I had known since I laid him there; and when at last I shouldered my knapsack and set forth again to battle with the world, I promised myself that, God willing, I would creep back to Rocca, when my days drew near to ending, and be buried by his side.

From hence, being, perhaps, a little less inclined than formerly for very distant parts, and willing to keep within reach of that grave, I went no further than Mantua, where I engaged myself as an engine-driver on the line, then not long completed, between that city and Venice. Somehow, although I had been trained to the working of engineering, I preferred in these days to earn my bread by driving. I liked the excitement of it, the sense of power, the rush of the air, the roar of the fire, the flitting of the landscape. Above all, I enjoyed to drive a night express. The worse the weather, the better it suited my sullen temper. For I was as hard, and harder than ever. The years had done nothing to soften me. They had only confirmed all that was blackest and bitterest in my heart.

I continued pretty faithful to the Mantua line, and had been working on it steadily for more than seven months when that which I am now about to relate took place.

It was in the month of March. The weather had been unsettled for some days past, and the nights stormy; and at one point along the line, near Ponte di Brenta, the waters had risen and swept away some seventy yards of embankment. Since this accident, the trains had all been obliged to stop at a certain spot between Padua and Ponte di Brenta, and the passengers, with their luggage, had thence to be transported in all kinds of vehicles, by a circuitous country road, to the nearest station on the other side of the gap, where another train and engine awaited them. This, of course, caused great confusion and annoyance, put all our time-tables wrong and subjected the public to a large amount of inconvenience. In the meanwhile an army of navvies was drafted to the spot, and worked day and night to repair the damage. At this time I was driving two through trains each day; namely, one from Mantua to Venice in the early morning, and a return train from Venice to Mantua in the afternoon—a tolerably full days' work, covering about one hundred and ninety miles of ground, and occupying between ten and eleven hours. I was therefore not best pleased when, on the third or fourth day after the accident, I was informed that, in addition to my regular allowance of work, I should that evening be required to drive a special train to Venice. This special train, consisting of an engine, a single carriage, and a break-van, was to leave the Mantua platform at eleven; at Padua the passengers were to alight and find post-chaises waiting to convey them to Ponte di Brenta; at Ponte di Brenta another engine, carriage, and break-van were to be in readiness; I was charged to accompany them throughout.

'Corpo di Bacco,' said the clerk who gave me my orders, 'you need not look so black, man. You are certain of a handsome gratuity. Do you know who goes with you?'

'Not I.'

'Not you, indeed! Why, it's the Duca Loredano, the Neapolitan ambassador.'

'Loredano!' I stammered. 'What Loredano? There was a Marchese —.'

'Certo. He was the Marchese Loredano some years ago; but he has come into his dukedom since then.'

'He must be a very old man by this time.'

'Yes, he is old; but what of that? He is as hale, and bright, and stately as ever. You have seen him before?'

'Yes,' I said, turning away; 'I have seen him—years ago.'

'You have heard of his marriage?'

I shook my head.

The clerk chuckled, rubbed his hands, and shrugged his

shoulders.

'An extraordinary affair,' he said. 'Made a tremendous esclandre at the time. He married his mistress—quite a common, vulgar girl—a Genoese—very handsome; but not received, of course. Nobody visits her.'

'Married her!' I exclaimed. 'Impossible.'

'True, I assure you.'

I put my hand to my head. I felt as if I had had a fall or a blow.

'Does she—does she go to-night?' I faltered.

'O dear, yes—she goes everywhere with him—never lets him out of her sight. You'll see her—la bella Duchessa!'

With this my informant laughed, and rubbed his hands again, and went back to his office.

The day went by, I scarcely know how, except that my whole soul was in a tumult of rage and bitterness. I returned from my afternoon's work about 7.25, and at 10.30 I was once again at the station. I had examined the engine; given instructions to the Fochista, or stoker, about the fire; seen to the supply of oil; and got all in readiness, when just as I was about to compare my watch with the clock in the ticket-office, a hand was laid upon my arm, and a voice in my ear said:

'Are you the engine-driver who is going on with this special train?'

I had never seen the speaker before. He was a small, dark man, muffled up about the throat, with blue glasses, a large black beard, and his hat drawn low upon his eyes.

'You are a poor man, I suppose,' he said, in a quick, eager whisper, 'and, like other poor men, would not object to be better off. Would you like to earn a couple of thousand florins?'

'In what way?'

'Hush! You are to stop at Padua, are you not, and to go on again at Ponte di Brenta?'

I nodded.

'Suppose you did nothing of the kind. Suppose, instead of turning off the steam, you jump off the engine, and let the train run on?'

'Impossible. There are seventy yards of embankment gone, and —.'

'Basta! I know that. Save yourself, and let the train run on. It would be nothing but an accident.'

I turned hot and cold; I trembled; my heart beat fast, and my breath failed.

'Why do you tempt me?' I faltered.

'For Italy's sake,' he whispered; 'for liberty's sake. I know you are no Italian; but, for all that, you may be a friend. This Loredano is one of his country's bitterest enemies. Stay, here are the two thousand florins.'

I thrust his hand back fiercely.

'No—no,' I said. 'No blood-money. If I do it, I do it neither for Italy nor for money; but for vengeance.'

'For vengeance!' he repeated.

At this moment the signal was given for backing up to the platform. I sprang to my place upon the engine without another word. When I again looked towards the spot where he had been standing, the stranger was gone.

I saw them take their places—Duke and Duchess, secretary and priest, valet and maid. I saw the station-master bow them into the carriage, and stand, bareheaded, beside the door. I could not distinguish their faces; the platform was too dusk, and the glare from the engine fire too strong; but I recognised her stately figure, and the poise of her head. Had I not been told who she was, I should have known her by those traits alone. Then the guard's whistle shrilled out, and the stationmaster made his last bow; I turned the steam on; and we started.

My blood was on fire. I no longer trembled or hesitated. I felt as if every nerve was iron, and every pulse instinct with deadly purpose. She was in my power, and I would be avenged. She should die—she, for whom I had stained my soul with my friend's blood! She should die, in the plentitude of her wealth and her beauty, and no power upon earth should save her!

The stations flew past. I put on more steam; I bade the fireman heap in the coke, and stir the blazing mass. I would have out-stripped the wind, had it been possible. Faster and faster—hedges and trees, bridges and stations, flashing past—villages no sooner seen than gone—telegraph wires twisting, and dipping, and twining themselves in one, with the awful swiftness of our pace! Faster and faster, till the fireman at my side looks white and scared, and refuses to add more fuel to the furnace. Faster and faster, till the wind rushes in our faces and drives the breath back upon our lips.

I would have scorned to save myself. I meant to die with the rest. Mad as I was—and believe from my very soul that I was utterly mad for the time—I felt a passing pang of pity for the old man and his suite. I would have spared the poor fellow at my side, too, if I could; but the pace at which we were going made escape impossible.

Vicenza was passed—a mere confused vision of lights. Pojana flew by. At Padua, but nine miles distant, our passengers were to alight. I saw the fireman's face turned upon me in remonstrance; I saw his lips move, though I could not hear a word; I saw his expression change suddenly from remonstrance to a deadly terror, and then—merciful Heaven! then, for the first time, I saw that he and I were no longer alone upon the engine.

There was a third man—a third man standing on my right hand, as the fireman was standing on my left—a tall, stalwart man, with short curling hair, and a flat Scotch cap upon his head. As I fell back in the first shock of surprise, he stepped nearer; took my place at the engine, and turned the steam off. I opened my lips to speak to him; he turned his head slowly, and looked me in the face.

Matthew Price!

I uttered one long wild cry, flung my arms wildly up above my head, and fell as if I had been smitten with an axe.

I am prepared for the objections that may be made to my story. I expect, as a matter of course, to be told that this was an optical illusion, or that I was suffering from pressure on the brain, or even that I laboured under an attack of temporary insanity. I have heard all these arguments before, and, if I may be forgiven for saying so, I have no desire to hear them again. My own mind has been made up upon this subject for many a year. All that I can say—all that I know is—that Matthew Price came back from the dead, to save my soul and the lives of those whom I, in my guilty rage, would have hurried to destruction. I believe this as I believe in the mercy of Heaven and the forgiveness of repentant sinners.

THE TUNNEL

Raymond Harvey

One Saturday night in October 1911, George Wilson, the stationmaster of Lintz Green Station on the Derwent Valley branch of the North Eastern Railway, Durham, saw the 10.45 train safely away and returned to his house. Before he could enter, a shot was heard by the departing passengers and a bullet penetrated through his left breast and flattened itself on the wall behind him. He died within minutes. The assailant of this sixty-year-old of a 'quiet inoffensive disposition' was never found but, strangely enough, it appears that sand had been thrown into his eyes before he was shot and a cloth gag was lying beside the body. Robbery might have been the motive, but his pockets only contained the coins from the booking-office sweet-meat machines and a little money of his own. He had no railway takings. He had no known enemies and the police search discovered a blank cartridge beside a nearby footpath.

It is from such inexplicable events that ghost stories grow. The line has since been closed down and the station is derelict, but some of the station houses, including the stationmaster's, continued to be used as private homes. Wilson's house was said to be haunted, and the sounds of a train travelling along the non-existent line could be heard above the blustering wind on stormy nights.

The events unfolded in The Tunnel *touches on one motive for murder and, with a fascinating inevitability, leads to a horrifying climax. But the real horror of the tunnel itself is not realised until the final paragraph.*

GEORGE WIGGS WAS just about to light his second cigarette when the small bell on the far wall of his signalbox shattered the silence. Although he had been a signalman now for over eight years, the sudden pinging of the warning bell still made him jump. Automatically he fished out his pocket watch and glanced at the hands. Hmm, the 12.18's early tonight, he thought to himself as he replaced his watch. Still, the goods trains usually were early or on time. It was always the passenger trains that were late and which made his job more difficult. He pushed himself up from the old armchair and taking up his large white duster, made his way over to the neat row of brass handles. Selecting the appropriate lever he wrapped his duster around the handle and with an experienced tug shifted the lever into the required position. This done he pressed the bell button to warn the next signalbox, then after writing the time in the log book returned to his armchair. Now for a quiet half hour, he thought to himself, knowing that the next train was not due until 12.45.

George settled down in the armchair and picked up the unlighted cigarette from the ashtray. Soon the blue tobacco smoke was curling into the air which was already laden with the smell of burning paraffin from the two bright lamps in the signalbox. Comfortable and content, George selected one of the colourful magazines from his pile on the floor. One of his first jobs when he came on duty was to unlock his cupboard and take out his pile of bright magazines. George was very proud of his collection, for all the magazines contained pin-up photographs of girls. George had soon realised that his job required a great deal of killing time in between trains and had found that studying colour pictures of naked females was a great help. Yet, as George gazed longingly at the picture of a large-breasted blonde girl emerging from the sea, he couldn't help comparing her with Veronica, his wife. Veronica may not be as well proportioned as this nymph of the sea, but she was just as pretty and her hair was just as blonde. But this nymph was smiling at him. Veronica didn't smile at him. This worried George. He realised that he and his wife had been steadily drifting apart in the last few years. He still loved Veronica deeply, but never seemed to get an opportunity of showing her. There was so much night-shift to do in his job and when he got home in the morning tired and ready for bed, Veronica would be getting up and starting her day. The only time he ever saw her really was from four o'clock to about nine o'clock in the evening when she always seemed to be busy doing some job or other and much too busy to spend time with George. On a few occasions he had put his arms around her while she was doing something around the house, only to be brushed away with an 'Oh, George, how do you expect me to do any work with you getting in the way,' or 'George, will you stop it and grow up.' Now he didn't try any more but contented himself with his pile of lovely girls, who always smiled at him and never told him to get out of the way or grow up.

Suddenly George jumped again. This time it was not the warning bell, but the jangling of his telephone bell that broke the silence. He closed his magazine and replaced it carefully on the pile. Now what was the matter, he wondered as he picked up the receiver.

'Hello, this is George Wiggs, box 172 speaking.'

'Hello, George. Harry here.' The voice of the chief controller crackled in his ear. 'Just ringing to tell you we've had a derailment. It's one helluva mess. Goods, not passengers, so no injuries, thank goodness.'

'Oh dear,' broke in George, 'how did it. . . .'

'Sorry, George. No time for details. Too much to be done. Just letting you know you can stand down for

tonight. I hope we'll be all clear by tomorrow. Goodnight.'
There was a sharp click and the line was dead. George replaced the receiver slowly. Well, well, a stand down. He took out his watch and saw it was only 12.35. If he got off as soon as possible he could be home before one o'clock. He gathered up his pile of magazines and locked them away. Then putting on his coat, he turned out the two oil lamps, locked the signalbox door and clip-clopped down the wooden steps.

The countryside was bathed in the pale white light of the full moon as he started his way home along the railway track. As the line would not be used that night he could take the short cut through Dingle tunnel. He strode briskly down the track, walking on the sleepers between the rails until at last he came to the dark cave-like opening of the tunnel. As he entered the tunnel the moonlight vanished and it was like leaving daylight and entering night, but he strode on confidently, having used this route many times in the past. Experience enabled him to pace his steps exactly from sleeper to sleeper although he could not see them. His footsteps echoed along the tunnel, together with the noise of tiny splashes as drips of water fell from the roof of the tunnel into the pools of stagnant water below. As he strode along he could hear the scratching patter of the rats as they scurried around in the tunnel searching for food. Here and there he could hear the rustling of paper as their sharp little teeth gnawed away at some scraps thrown from a passing train. Every now and then he would hiss out a 'shoo gerraway', and listen to their claws scampering on the cinders. Then he was out in the clean moonlight again and able to see where he was going.

The church clock was striking one o'clock as he turned down his street. He was thinking how Veronica would feel having him home in bed with her. She would be in bed by now. He would go up quietly, undress and then kiss her gently. She would wake up and he would make love to her and they would be blissfully happy. His stride quickened as his imagination created the scene for him. He did love Veronica so deeply and he did want her so much. He quietly opened the gate and closed it behind him. Then to his amazement he saw the dark hulk of a motor-bike in the pathway leaning against the wall. He looked at the number plate and recognised it as the bike of one of his best friends, Stephen Hollins, but what on earth was it doing here at this time? Puzzled he went to the back door and slipped his key into the lock. He quietly opened and closed the door and sat down on the floor to take off his shoes. All he could hear was his own heavy breathing after the brisk walk home.

The house was dark and quiet, but he could find his way around with his eyes shut. He crept silently up the stairs and tiptoed along the passage to the bedroom door. Before he reached the door his body froze. Faintly the voices floated from the bedroom. 'Kiss me again, Steve. Oh, darling, kiss me.' It was Veronica's voice and intermingled with it were the deep grunts of a man's voice, 'Love you, love you.'

George was dazed as he crept to the doorway. The door was half open and he could see the large mirror of his wife's dressing table. Reflected in the mirror and bathed in white moonlight lay the naked bodies of his wife and Stephen Hollins. Veronica's body looked like a white marble statue lying there, while the darker body of Stephen lay more in the shadow. But George could see quite clearly the heads locked in a passionate kiss, while Stephen's dark hand caressed the white moonlit body of his wife. The dark hand fascinated George; he watched its every move and the more it caressed her naked flesh the more he hated it. George knew if he watched much more he would charge in and kill both of them there and then, but instant death would be too good for them; they must suffer for this and suffer they would. George left the house as silently as he had entered and made his way back to the signalbox for the night, and every step of the way back his plan became clearer and clearer, and when he finally reached the box, he was actually smiling.

George returned home at his usual time and was careful to behave exactly as he normally did. He went to bed at the usual time and got up at 3.30 p.m. when Veronica called him. After his meal he went to get some more of the pills that the doctor had prescribed to help him sleep and then packed his sandwich box as usual. At seven o'clock he told Veronica that he had dropped in to see Stephen while he was out. He watched her face carefully as he was talking to her, but apart from the fact that she avoided his eyes while she spoke, she covered up very well.

'What did you want to see Stephen for?' she asked, pretending to be looking for something in a drawer.

'Oh, just to ask him to bring you over to the signalbox at 10.30 this evening,' he answered casually. Veronica looked at him for the first time since Stephen's name had been mentioned.

'What on earth do I want to go over to your silly little box at 10.30 for, may I ask?' she said sarcastically.

'It's a big surprise, dear,' he said smiling at her. 'I can't tell you yet, but I know it will make you very happy.' Veronica did not answer back but looked very puzzled. 'Well, will you come, darling?' he asked.

'What did Stephen say?' she asked cautiously.

'Why, he said he'd come with you with pleasure,' answered George.

'Oh, very well then, but I'm not staying long, mind, and you'd better not be wasting my time.'

'I wouldn't dream of dragging you over for nothing, dear, you know that,' said George soothingly. Veronica grunted and went about her work again.

That evening when he started his shift, George did not unlock his magazine cupboard as usual but took out three china tea mugs and poured some milk into each one. Then he took some tablets from a little brown bottle and dropped them in two of the mugs. He got the primus stove working and put the kettle on. When Veronica and Stephen appeared at the door of the signalbox, he was just pouring the boiling water into the teapot.

'Ah, here you are,' he said cheerfully, 'just in time for a cup of tea.' Veronica and Stephen sat down without comment, while George fussed around trying to make them feel at home.

'Now, shall I be mother?' he laughed as he poured the

steaming tea into the three mugs.

'Help yourselves to sugar.' He pushed forward the tin box. 'Here we are; the mugs with handles for guests, the one without for me.'

'Now look here, George. We didn't come all the way over here at this time of night, just to play tea parties with you.' Veronica's eyes flashed as she spoke. 'You said you had some. . . .'

'Patience, my dear,' interrupted George, 'all in good time. Just relax, drink your tea and make yourselves at home.'

Veronica and Stephen exchanged a quick glance, then settled back with their tea. While they were drinking, George pretended to be too busy to talk, and fussed around the signalbox looking in books and pretending to check everything. At last, he settled down and drank his tea.

'Now,' he said, 'my good news is that I have been promoted to a bigger box in the North of England.' He paused and watched his wife and her lover, then continued, 'We get a house supplied, so as we will not be seeing Stephen any more I thought it a good idea to have this little farewell tea party.' He beamed across at them. Veronica looked stunned. She gazed at Stephen, not knowing what to say.

'Well, isn't anyone going to congratulate me, then?' asked George with a smile. Veronica and Stephen were too busy looking at each other in desperation to congratulate him.

'Well, dear me,' continued George, 'anyone would think you didn't want me to get this job, dear. Are you sure you wouldn't rather stay with Stephen? I can go on my own if you like.' He waited for her reply. Veronica seemed to have difficulty in thinking. She was holding her head and her eyes looked very tired.

'I don't want to go to . . . to . . . to . . .' but that was all she said before her head slumped to one side of the armchair.

'Veronica, what is it?' Stephen asked getting to his feet and bending over her. But he seemed to lose his balance and toppled head first to the floor and lay in a heap where he had fallen. George's smile widened. 'Yes, I knew you wanted to be together, my dears, so together you shall be.'

He went to his cupboard and took out a coil of wire and a lantern. He placed the articles on the table and then began to undress his wife.

Stephen felt the sting of cold water on his face and opened his eyes. He was lying inside a railway tunnel with George Wiggs standing over him with a lantern. He felt cold and stiff and tried to get up.

'Sorry, Stephen, old chap, but I'm afraid you can't get up. You see, I've tied you down with wire.' Stephen screwed his eyes around and saw that his wrists and ankles were securely tied with wire in such a way that his arms and legs were spreadeagled across the railway lines.

'Yes, Stephen,' said George, realising Stephen had seen his plight, 'when the train comes along it will sever both feet just above the ankles and both hands and arms nearly to the elbows.'

'You madman,' cried Stephen, 'you can't do this! Let me go at once. Get this wire off, do you hear me?'

'Yes, I hear you, Stephen, but I'm just making sure your dirty little hands don't touch my wife any more.' George grinned down at him.

'Clever, don't you think, Stephen, and if you concentrate you should be able to feel Veronica's feet with your feet, you see she's in exactly the same dilemma as you are.'

Stephen craned his head and gazed down over his own naked body towards his feet and there he saw the naked spreadeagled body of Veronica. So that was the plan; the train would pass over both of them and just cut off their arms and feet so that they died slowly in great pain. He dropped his head back exhausted.

'Please listen, George, I'll do anything you say, just. . . .'

'Sorry, old chap,' said George, 'but you're wasting your time. I've got to go now, anyway, so I'll just wake Veronica, and then I'll leave you two lovebirds to it.'

With that, he splashed some water over Veronica,

waited until she opened her eyes, then said:

'Goodbye, Veronica. I hope you and your lover will be very happy for the next ten minutes.'

Then he picked up his lantern and crunched his way back along the cinders towards the signal box.

In the feeble glow of moonlight that reached them from the mouth of the tunnel, Veronica twisted her head to try and understand what was happening. She babbled a stream of questions to Stephen and when she got the answers, she just screamed at the top of her voice to George to come and set her free, but George did not come. He was too busy making a bonfire with two piles of clothes behind the signalbox. Even while she was screaming at the top of her voice, Stephen could hear the distant rumble of the approaching train. He tugged with his arms and legs, but the wire merely bit deeper into the flesh. He looked along the tunnel in time to see the front lights of the train flashing down towards them. The tracks were trembling beneath his legs and arms now, and Veronica's screams filled his ears with the roar of the engine. He pressed his head back, closed his eyes and felt his body stiffen in anticipation.

Two red-hot knives seemed to slice through his legs, then his arms, while all around, thunder seemed to be crashing at him. Then the thunder rolled away into the distance. He was aware of a burning pain in his arms and legs. He opened his eyes weakly and looked at the horrible little stumps that twitched just below each elbow. He clumsily propped himself up on his left elbow and saw his legs now came to dark points, while on either side of the rails an array of feet and forearms with open hands lay strewn about. Veronica groaned, then remembering what had just happened began screaming again as she saw the severed parts of her body. Stephen knew that they were both bleeding badly now, but would probably suffer this horrible pain for a long time before death finally came.

Veronica was beside herself now, calling George every name she could think of in between her wild screaming fits. Stephen realised there was only one way out for them. In extreme pain he worked his way on his bleeding stumps over to her, then wrapping the remains of his arms around her neck, he dragged her head round and placed it over the sticky rail. Then he placed his head over and tried to hold her still as best he could. He hoped that the wait for the next train would not be too long and when it came it would sever off the heads cleanly so that they would die quickly.

While they waited lying in the warm pool of their mingling bloods, their attention was distracted by the long dark shapes that scurried round them, slowly getting nearer. Suddenly Veronica shrieked as a long fat rat began gnawing at her right foot, which was a about a yard from her face. Other rats then closed in to start nibbling at other parts of severed limbs that lay around. Stephen tried to grip her to comfort her, but by now she was raving away to herself. Suddenly, she began complaining of the pain in her ankles getting worse. Stephen could think of nothing to say in comfort to her when he looked over his shoulder down at her legs and to his horror saw two black shapes pulling and chewing at the stumps of her legs. He threw his right leg across hers and the shapes scuttled back into the shadows. Then under his throat he felt the rail vibrate and he knew the end would soon come. He made sure her neck was also on the trembling rail, then closed his eyes. He felt her body stiffen against his as the roar of the train approached. He felt her firm breasts press against his body, then a great white light flashed through his head—then darkness.

THE EIGHTH LAMP

Roy Vickers

Charles Dickens would have known the first London 'tube' railway even though we have no record that he actually travelled in it. It was the Tower Hill subway, completed in 1870, which was a bored circular tunnel (a true tube rather than a 'cut and cover' tunnel), lined with cast-iron and shield-driven under the Thames to the opposite bank. This, and the subsequent City and South London Railway, being three miles long and having five stations when opened in 1890, must have opened new vistas of Hell to the nervous traveller.

The words underground *and* underworld *are often synonymous and both are associated with death and burial, especially in connection with a grim afterlife. Because of this, the London Underground Railway has, in the imagination of a number of authors, become an ideal setting for stories of the macabre.*

To enter the classical underworld it was necessary for Charon, the boatman, to ferry you over the river Styx; but in The Eighth Lamp *Roy Vickers provides a much more modern and logical means of entry.*

WITH A MUFFLED, metallic roar the twelve-forty-five, the last train on the Underground, lurched into Cheyne Road station. A small party of belated theatre-goers alighted; the sleepy guard blew his whistle, and the train rumbled on its way to the outlying suburbs.

A couple of minutes later, signalman George Raoul emerged from the tunnel, swung himself on to the up-platform and switched off the nearest lamp. Simultaneously a door in the wall on the down-side opened and the stationmaster appeared.

'Nothing to report, Mr Jenkins,' said Raoul. He spoke in an ordinary speaking voice, but in the dead silence of the station his words carried easily across the rails—words that were totally untrue. He had something of considerable importance to report, but he knew that if he were to make that report he would probably be marked down as unfit for night duty, and he could not afford to risk that at present.

'All right, George. Good night.'

'G'night, Mr Jenkins.'

Raoul passed down the length of the up-platform, dousing each light as he came to the switch. Then he dropped onto the track, crossed and made for the farthest switch on the down-platform.

Cheyne Road station was wholly underground—it was but an enlarged strip of tunnel—and the lighting regulations did not apply to it. There were eight lamps on each platform.

The snap of the switch echoed in the deserted station like the crack of a pistol. Raoul started. The silence that followed gripped him. Pulling himself together he hurried on to the second switch.

'Ugh!'

By the third lamp he stopped and shuddered as his eye fell upon a recruiting poster. In the gloom the colouring of the poster was lost—some crudity in the printing asserted itself—and the beckoning smile of a young soldier seemed like the mirthless grin of a death mask. And the death mask was just like —.

'You're all right,' he assured himself aloud. 'It's the new station that's doing it.'

Yes, it was the new station that was doing it. But he would not grumble on that account. It was a bit of rare luck, being transferred from Baker Street—just when he was transferred. For all its familiarity, he could never have stood night-work at Baker Street—now.

Even after three weeks in the new signalbox he could never pass a Circle train without a faint shudder. The Circle trains had a morbid fascination for him. They passed you on the down-line. Half a dozen stations and they would be pulling up at Baker Street. Then on through the tunnel and, in about an hour, back they came past your box and still on the down-line. In the Circle trains his half-nurtured imagination saw something ruthless and inevitable—something vaguely connected with fate and eternity and things like that.

His mind had momentarily wandered so that he took the fourth switch unconsciously. As he made for the fifth, his nerve again faltered.

'Didn't ought to have taken on this extra work,' he seemed to shout into the dark mouth of the tunnel.

''Tain't worth it for three bob. It's the cleaner's job by rights.'

Yes, it was the cleaner's job by rights. But the cleaner was an old man, unreliable for night-work; and when the stationmaster had offered Raoul the job of 'clearing up last thing' for three shillings a week, he had jumped at it. The three shillings would make life perceptibly brighter for Jinny—her new life with him.

Between the fifth lamp and the sixth was the stationmaster's den. On a nail outside the door hung the keys with which Raoul would presently lock the ticket-barrier and the outer door of the booking office.

He snatched the keys as he passed and then, as if to humanise the desolation, he broke into a piercing, tuneless whistle that carried him to the seventh lamp.

A trifling mechanical difficulty with the seventh switch was enough to check the whistling. For a moment he stood motionless in the silence—the silence that seemed to come out of the tunnel like a dank mist and envelop him. He measured the distance to the switch of the eighth lamp. The switch of the eighth lamp was by the foot of the staircase. He need scarcely stop as he turned it—and then he would let himself take the staircase two, three, four steps at a time.

Click!

The eighth lamp was extinguished. From the ticket-office on the street level a single ray of light made blacker the darkness of the station. But Raoul, within a couple of feet of the staircase, waited, crouching.

His hand clutched the stair-rail and he twisted his body round so that he could look up the line. He could not see more than a few feet in front of him, but he could hear, distinct and unmistakable, the rumbling murmur of an approaching train.

All his instincts as a railway man told him that his senses were deceiving him. The twelve-forty-five was the last train down—and he and the stationmaster had together seen it through. There were a dozen reasons why it would be impossible for another train to run without previous notification to the signalling staff. And yet—the rumbling was growing momentarily louder. The air, driven through the tunnel before the advancing train, was blowing like a breeze upon his face.

Louder and louder grew the rumbling until it rose to the familiar roar. In another second he would see the lights.

But there were no lights. The train lurched and clattered through the station and was swallowed up in the downside tunnel. There were no lights, but Raoul had seen that it was a Circle train.

For a nightmare eternity he seemed to be rushing with gigantic strides up an endless staircase—across a vast hall that had once been a ticket-office, and then:

'Hi! Where yer comin' to?'

The raucous indignation of the night constable, into whom he had cannoned, recalled him to sanity.

'Sorry, mate!' he panted. 'I didn't see you—as I come by.'

'Call that comin' by?' demanded the constable. 'Why, you was running like a house afire! What's going on down there, then?'

'Nothing,' retorted Raoul.

The constable, unsatisfied, walked through the ticket-office and peered over the barrier. The silence and the darkness gave him a hint.

'Bit lonesome down there, last thing, ain't it?' he suggested.

'Yes,' grunted Raoul, as he locked the barrier, 'somethin' chronic.'

'I know,' said the constable. He had not been on night-duty for ten years without learning the meaning of nerves.

A short chat with the constable served to restore Raoul's balance, after which he locked up as usual and made his way to the tenement he shared with Jinny, resolving that this time he would report the occurrence to the station-master on the following day.

During their three weeks' occupation of the tenement Jinny had made a practice of waiting up to give him his supper. As he came in she was lying asleep, half-dressed, in the second-hand upholstered armchair that had been theirs for three weeks.

'Hullo, Jinny!' he called, with intentional loudness. He wanted to wake her up thoroughly so that she would chatter to him.

'Blessed if I hadn't dropped off!' she exclaimed by way of apology, as she hastily got up and busied herself with his cocoa.

'There's no need for you to wait up, you know, Jinny,' he said, as he seated himself at the table. 'Only I'm not denying as I'm glad to see you a bit before we turn in.'

'Funny thing 'appened tonight,' he went on. 'After I'd seen the twelve-forty-five through and Mr Jenkins 'ad gone and I'd nearly finished turnin' off the lights —.'

He told the whole story jovially, jauntily, as if it were a rather good joke. He attained a certain vividness of expression which only became blurred at that part which dealt with his own sensations after the passing of the train.

The woman was wide awake before he had finished. All her life she had indirectly depended on the Underground railway, and knew its workings almost as well as the signalman himself.

'Arf a mo', George!' she said, as he finished. 'How did it get past the signal if you was out of your box?'

'That's what beats me!' exclaimed George Raoul, thumping the table as if herein lay the very cream of the joke.

She looked at him with the dawning suspicion that he had been drinking; but as she looked she knew that he had not.

'What sort o' train was it?' she asked; keeping her eyes fixed on his.

For a moment he did not reply. His gaze dwelt on his cocoa as he answered:

'Circle train.'

Jinny made no reply, and the subject was dropped.

An hour later neither of them was asleep.

'Jinny,' said Raoul, 'what yer thinkin' about?'

'Nothing,' she retorted, and her voice came sulkily through the darkness.

'Go on. Out with it!'

'All right! 'Ave it your own way, an' don't blame me. I was wonderin' what Pete was doin' now—this minute.'

'Pete!' echoed Raoul, through teeth that chattered, though he tried to clench them. 'You've no call to wonder about 'im—not after the way he served you, his lawful, wedded wife.'

'I didn't mean to,' she defended herself; 'only you tellin' me about that train—and 'im being a Circle driver—set me off.'

'You've no call to think about 'im,' repeated Raoul doggedly. 'You can lay he ain't thinkin' about you—'e's thinkin' about the woman he left you for.'

There was a moment's silence, and then:

'P'r'aps—and p'r'aps not,' replied Jinny.

On the following morning Raoul decided that he would still say nothing to the stationmaster about the train that had followed the twelve-forty-five.

The position was by no means an easy one. He knew that his nerves would not stand the strain of turning out the lights on the platform—not yet awhile, anyhow. On the other hand, he dared not throw up his job. During the last three weeks he had seen something of Jinny's nature; and although his animal love for her had in no way abated, he had a pretty shrewd suspicion that she would not face even temporary destitution with him.

After much deliberation, he hit on a comparatively neat compromise. As he left home to go on duty he approached an elderly loafer leaning against the wall of a public house near the station.

'Suppose you don't want a tanner a night for five minutes' work as a child could do?' he suggested.

'All accordin' to what the work is,' answered the loafer.

'Turnin' off the lights mostly,' said Raoul. 'Anyway, if you want the job 'ang about 'ere'—indicating the station— 'at twelve-forty-five sharp until you see the stationmaster come off. Then 'op into the station. You'll find me on the platform.'

'I'm doing this on me own,' he added. 'My missis likes me to be 'ome early, and it's worth a tanner a night for a bit of 'elp. See?'

The loss of the extra three shillings a week, Raoul decided, could safely be ascribed to an act of war economy on the part of the railway company. Better lose three bob a week than have to chuck up your job, he reasoned.

The services of the loafer proved a wise investment. Raoul showed him where to find the switches. On the first night he explained it all over and over again, glancing from time to time towards the tunnel, thereby extracting full value for his sixpence.

The explanation finished, and while three lamps remained burning, he left the loafer for a suddenly remembered duty on the ticket-office level. Thence, in a comfortable circle of light, he presently called:

'Turn off them last three lights, mate, and come up.'

The loafer sluggishly obeyed, and then shambled up the staircase to receive the most easily earned sixpence of his life.

'Same time tomorrer night if you're on,' said Raoul.

'I'm on right enough,' replied the loafer.

That formula was repeated every night for some half-a-dozen nights. Then came a night on which the loafer failed to appear.

For five minutes Raoul waited. He went up to the street level and looked round. The station was deserted—there was not even a constable on point duty.

When the loafer's defection became obvious, Raoul's first thought was to leave the lights burning and go straight home. Reflection showed that this would mean the sack—which in turn would mean the probable loss of Jinny—the loss of that for which the very agonies he was now enduring had been incurred.

Besides, there was another thought that drove him back into the station. Somehow or other he would be compelled to explain why he had left the lights burning—why he had been afraid to return to the station. They would ask questions. And God knew where those questions might lead!

The up-platform presented no terrors. On the down-platform—in the moment of utter darkness when the eighth lamps was extinguished—he knew that his fear would reach its zenith.

And precisely at that moment the distant rumbling in the tunnel began—the driven air, like a breeze, played about his temples.

He could not prevent his eyes from staring in the direction of the tunnel. He tried to move backwards up the staircase, but all power of voluntary action had left him.

The train seemed to slacken speed as it rolled into the

83

station. As it came towards him, slowly and more slowly, his eyes were glued to a faint luminosity in the driver's window—a luminosity that gathered shape as it came nearer and nearer.

'Pete!' he gasped—and with that conscious effort of the muscles his brain regained control of his body and he rushed up the stairs, uncertain whether the train had stopped—knowing that if it came again it would stop and wait for him.

Jinny was awake and moving about the room when he returned. She glanced at his drawn face and knew what had happened.

'Seen it again?' she asked.

'Wot if I have?' he demanded.

'Nothing,' she retorted.

She waited while he ate his supper in silence.

'George,' she said, as he put down his cup for the last time.

'Well?'

'Suppose we know for certain as Pete was dead'—she paused, but did not know enough to look at his mouth, and his eyes were turned from her—'Why, then we—we could get spliced proper, couldn't we?'

Still avoiding her gaze he nodded.

'Suppose,' she said, leaning across the table until her elbows touched his, 'suppose we was to go about the banns tomorrer?'

Only then did Raoul look up and meet the woman's gaze. In her eye there was nothing of accusation. But there was nothing of doubt.

'Right-o!' he said.

On the following morning they went together to the parish chuch and, being recommended thence to the vicarage, explained their needs. They learnt that they would have to wait for three Sundays before they could be married.

He was gloomy and depressed as they left the vicarage.

'Three weeks'll soon pass,' she said, as if to console him.

'Aye,' he grunted.

'An' you'll feel a lot better when it's done,' she added.

To this he made no reply, and she did not labour the point. Indeed, it was the last veiled allusion she ever made to the subject.

On his way to the station he came across the loafer in the usual place outside the public-house. The man shambled towards him ready with an excuse, but Raoul cut him short.

'Shan't be wantin' you no more,' he said gruffly, and thereby burnt his boats behind him.

During the hours that passed between his going on duty in the early afternoon and leaving the box after the passing of the twelve-forty-five, he did not once repent having dispensed with the services of the loafer. True, his mind dwelt almost continuously on the ordeal before him. But Jinny had unconsciously given him a weapon when she had told him he would feel better when it was done.

That night, as he doused the eighth lamp, he turned and faced the tunnel.

'I'm actin' square by 'er now, ain't I?' he shouted.

Then, for all the furious beating of his heart, he walked at a leisurely pace up the staircase, and so, completing his duties, into the street.

On the next night it was easier, and, with each night that brought his marriage nearer, his confidence grew. His nerve would falter sometimes, but always he managed to ascend the staircase one step at at time. Jinny was a secret tower of strength to him—so that all went reasonably well with him until, by the merest accident, the tower of strength crumbled.

Three Sundays had passed since their visit to the vicarage when the accident happened. The accident took the form of his meeting Mabel Owen as he was returning home from duty.

He had known Mabel in the Baker Street days before he had known Jinny—a fact of which Jinny was well aware. Mabel was returning from some unmentioned errand in the West End when she ran into him and exclaimed:

'Blessed if it ain't George Raoul! 'Ow goes it, George? Seems ages since we met, don't it! An' what might you be doin' in these parts?'

'I work over 'ere now,' explained Raoul. 'Cheyne Road. 'Ow goes it with you?'

Then, because he had no wish to appear churlish to a girl with whom he had once walked out, he invited her to an adjacent coffee stall.

He arrived at the tenement barely half an hour later than usual. But that half-hour was more than enough for Jinny.

'You're late, George,' she said, as he came in.

'Sorry, Jinny,' he replied. 'Couldn't help myself. Met a friend as I was comin' off. Had to say a civil word to 'er.'

'*Er!*' repeated Jinny.

'Mabel Owen,' he said—and his clumsy effort to say it casually fanned her suspicion.

'Oh!' shrilled Jinny. 'So you keep me waitin' while you go gallivantin' about with that dressed up bit o' damaged goods!'

'You've no right to say that of Mabel,' protested Raoul.

'No right!' she echoed. 'Oh no! I've no right to say that of 'er, me livin' with you with no weddin'-ring as you've given me. No better than 'er, I'm not. And don't you let me forget it neither, George Raoul!'

'Stow that, Jinny!' he commanded, with rising anger. 'Ain't we fixed it up to get spliced proper day after tomorrer?'

The glint in his eye, partly of anger but partly also of fear, restrained her from further outburst and drove her indignation inwards so that she sulked.

She was still sulking on the following day, compelling him to eat his midday meal in gloomy silence, wherefore he left home for work sooner than was necessary.

He was in the signalbox before he recognised that the secret tower of strength had crumbled as a result of the accident of his meeting with Mabel Owen. Jinny had shown him a side of her nature that had been conspicuously absent in the earlier stages of his infatuation. And now his life was to become irrevocably linked with hers.

With the first taste of the bitterness of his sin came remorse; and with remorse came, with renewed strength, the terror which he had partly beaten back.

The terror began to grip him even before the station-master had left. In the signalbox he had formed the plan of telling the stationmaster that he could not turn out the lights that night—that he must hurry to the bedside of a dying child—any lie would provided it saved him for that night. Tomorrow night he would be married to Jinny. He would have made what reparation lay in his power and would feel the safer.

'Good night, George.'

'G'night, Mr Jenkins.'

The stationmaster hung the keys on the nail outside his den and walked off. Raoul would have called after him, but checked himself. The stationmaster would not believe that lie about the dying child. His face would betray his terror—his terror of the tunnel. The stationmaster would ask him why he was afraid of the tunnel, and—God knew where those questions would lead!

'Funny, it's worse'n ever to-night!' he said, as he finished the lights on the up-platform—for he was not analytical and did not wholly understand why the secret tower of strength had crumbled. He only knew that he did not want to marry Jinny on the following day.

He only now saw his sin in gaining possession of her— in the way that he had gained possession of her—in its naked hideousness.

The odd fatalism of his class prevented him from shirking the lights on the down-platform. What has to be will be. The same fatalism drove him ultimately to dousing the eighth lamp and turning, like a doomed rat, to face the already rumbling horror of the tunnel.

More slowly than before, as if it knew that he must wait for it, the train came on. Then in his ears sounded the familiar grinding of the brakes.

The train had stopped in the station. The faint luminosity in the driver's window grinned its welcome. Then it beckoned.

'I'm comin', Pete.'

From the corner by the staircase, where he had been crouching, he moved across the platform and boarded the train.

Dawn, breaking over the serried roofs of Chelsea, found
Jinny sitting wide-eyed before the untouched meal she
had prepared hours ago for Raoul.

As if the first faint streaks of light ended her vigil she
dropped her face on her arms and burst into tears.

'Fool that I was! Why couldn't I 'ave 'eld me jore about
Mabel Owen till we was spliced proper? And now he's left
me, and Pete—.'

The passion of weeping rose to its height, spent itself,
and left her in another mood.

'E needn't think 'e can get away as easy as all that,' she
muttered savagely. 'If I'm a fool, he's a worse one—as 'e'll
soon find to 'is cost.'

At eight o'clock she washed herself and donned her
black dress. Thus arrayed as a respectable woman of the
working-class she made her way to the nearest police
station and asked for the Inspector.

'I'm Mrs Pete Comber,' she explained. 'My husband
used to be a driver on the Underground. Circle train, he
druv.'

'Well?' said the Inspector.

She did not hesitate in her confession. She had weighed
the cost of her revenge, and did not shrink from paying it.

'A man called George Raoul used to lodge with us—a
signaller, 'e was, and worked at Baker Street. Me and 'im
got friendly, if you understand, only I wouldn't 'ave
anything to do with him while I was livin' with my
'usband, not being that sort.

'Bout a couple of months ago George come to me and
says, "Jinny," he says, "you won't see Pete no more," he
says. "Why not?" I says. "Chucked up his job and
everythink," he says; "met him when we was bein' paid,"
he says, "an' he asked me to tell you quite friendly like,"
he says.'

'Look here,' interrupted the Inspector, 'we can't have
anything to do with all this.'

'You wait,' replied Jinny, scarcely noticing the interrup-
tion. 'As soon as George told me, I was that wild with my

'usbin that I let George take me off—me that had always been a respectable woman. Never entered my 'ead as he wasn't tellin' the truth. Next day George was turned on to Cheyne Road an' we come to live up 'ere.

'Well, first he begun tellin' me as he'd bin seein' things on the Underground. That started me thinkin'. I can put two an' two together, same as anyone else, an' I started takin' notice of what he was talking about in 'is sleep. And I tell you as sure as I stand here, George Raoul killed my 'usbin, and I dessay 'e's put im in one of the old holes in the Baker Street tunnel wot they used for storin' the tools.'

The Inspector began to take notes and to ask a number of questions. Of one thing only was he sure—that the woman before him was giving a genuine expression of opinion.

'And now George has left you, I suppose, and that's why you've come along to us?' he suggested.

'He has left me,' replied the woman. 'But I only found all this out properly night before last, an' I couldn't be sure. I'd have come along 'ere any'ow.'

The Inspector guessed that the last statement was a lie. But unless the man, when they caught him, definitely implicated the woman he knew that the Crown would not prosecute her.

'All right,' he said. 'We'll find George for you. Leave your address and call here to-morrow.'

The Inspector, after instructing a plain-clothes man to shadow Jinny to her home, went to interview the Cheyne Road stationmaster.

On the following morning, when Jinny called at the police station, she was asked to examine a suit of clothing, a pocket knife, and a greasy case containing a number of small personal papers and other belongings.

'Yes, they're Pete's right enough, pore dear!' she exclaimed, and then burst into a flood of maudlin tears.

The Inspector waited unmoved. He believed not at all in the genuineness of Jinny's grief; but convention had its claims, and he said nothing until the storm of tears had subsided.

'Now, Mrs Comber,' he said presently, 'I want you to

dry your face and come along o' me.

'It's all right,' he added. 'Nothing's going to happen to you.'

He took her for some distance in a taxi-cab to a low, vault-like building near the river. There, after parley with the local officials, he led her to an inner room.

'Steady now,' he warned her. 'We're going to show you a dead body.'

Someone removed a cloth, and at the same moment the Inspector demanded:

'Who's that?'

'George Raoul!' gasped Jinny.

As the Inspector, taking her by the arm, led her from the room a question forced itself to her lips.

'You—you ain't 'ung him already?'

'No,' replied the Inspector, with a grim laugh, 'we ain't 'ung him. Wasn't needed. We found your husband in that disused hole, same as you said—and we found George Raoul alongside him—like that. Heart failure, the doctor says. Funny thing! As far as I can make out, he must have been skeered or something and run all the way through the tunnel from Cheyne Street to Baker Street where he done it. Must have been the running as did for his heart!'

That at any rate, was the explanation based on the Coroner's Court.

THE COMPENSATION HOUSE

Charles Collins

Railway architecture has many interesting aspects. We wonder at the vast viaducts thrown over wide valleys and bridges over deep gorges. We are fascinated by the ramps, sheds, round-houses, sidings with their humps and inclined planes, culverts, pumping stations—a tremendous variety of ingenious methods of overcoming problems of terrain or traffic-handling. The stations and nearby houses and buildings are a subject of study in themselves and if we imagine them in the dim gas-light of their heyday we may well wonder what went on behind their closed doors and shutters.

Charles Alston Collins (1828–73) was the younger brother of Wilkie Collins the well-known writer of macabre short stories and novels. In 1860 Charles married Kate the youngest daughter of Charles Dickens and became a contributor of essays and stories to All The Year Round. He suffered from ill-health and was of a nervous disposition, being particularly fearful of ghosts. It is told that when he was staying near Ewell in 1851 it was necessary for him to walk home alone from the railway station on a dark October night. The night noises and darkness so affected his sensitive imagination that he went into a state of panic, which was happily relieved when he met his friend John Millais who had set out to find him. 'I gave myself up for lost,' he said, 'what I have suffered is beyond conception.'

For his contribution to the 1866 Christmas issue, Charles Collins turned his attention to a building at Mugby Junction and the powers of imagination that were able to frighten himself were turned to you, the reader.

'THERE'S NOT A looking-glass in all the house, sir. It's some peculiar fancy of my master's. There isn't one in any single room in the house.'

It was a dark and gloomy-looking building, and had been purchased by this Company for an enlargement of their Goods Station. The value of the house had been referred to what was popularly called 'a compensation jury,' and the house was called, in consequence, The Compensation House. It had become the Company's property; but its tenant still remained in possession, pending the commencement of active building operations. My attention was originally drawn to this house because it stood directly in front of a collection of huge pieces of timber which lay near this part of the Line, and on which I sometimes sat for half an hour at a time, when I was tired by my wanderings about Mugby Junction.

It was square, cold, grey-looking, built of rough-hewn stone, and roofed with thin slabs of the same material. Its windows were few in number, and very small for the size of the building. In the great blank, grey broadside, there were only four windows. The entrance-door was in the middle of the house; there was a window on either side of it, and there were two more in the single story above. The blinds were all closely drawn, and when the door was shut, the dreary building gave no sign of life or occupation.

But the door was not always shut. Sometimes it was opened from within, with a great jingling of bolts and door-chains, and then a man would come forward and stand upon the doorstep, snuffing the air as one might do who was ordinarily kept on rather a small allowance of that element. He was stout, thickset, and perhaps fifty or sixty years old—a man whose hair was cut exceedingly close, who wore a large bushy beard, and whose eye had a sociable twinkle in it which was prepossessing. He was dressed, whenever I saw him, in a greenish-brown frock-coat made of some material which was not cloth, wore a waistcoat and trousers of light colour, and had a frill to his shirt—an ornament, by the way, which did not seem to go at all well with the beard, which was continually in contact with it. It was the custom of this worthy person, after standing for a short time on the threshold inhaling the air, to come forward into the road, and, after glancing at one of the upper windows in a half mechanical way, to cross over to the logs, and, leaning over the fence which guarded the railway, to look up and down the Line (it passed before the house) with the air of a man accomplishing a self-imposed task of which nothing was expected to come. This done, he would cross the road again, and turning on the threshold to take a final sniff of air, disappeared once more within the house, bolting and chaining the door again as if there were no probability of its being reopened for at least a week. Yet half an hour had not passed before he was out in the road again, sniffing the air and looking up and down the Line as before.

It was not very long before I managed to scrape acquaintance with this restless personage. I soon found out that my friend with the shirt-frill was the confidential servant, butler, valet, factotum, what you will, of a sick gentleman, a Mr Oswald Strange, who had recently come to inhabit the house opposite, and concerning whose history my new acquaintance, whose name I ascertained was Masey, seemed disposed to be somewhat communicative. His master, it appeared, had come down to this place, partly for the sake of reducing his establishment—not, Mr Masey was swift to inform me, on economical principles, but because the poor gentleman, for particular reasons, wished to have few dependents about him—partly in order that he might be near his old friend, Dr Garden, who was established in the neighbourhood,

94

and whose society and advice were necessary to Mr Strange's life. That life was, it appeared, held by this suffering gentleman on a precarious tenure. It was ebbing away fast with each passing hour. The servant already spoke of his master in the past tense, describing him to me as a young gentleman not more than five-and-thirty years of age, with a young face, as far as the features and build of it went, but with an expression which had nothing of youth about it. This was the great peculiarity of the man. At a distance he looked younger than he was by many years, and strangers, at the time when he had been used to get about, always took him for a man of seven or eight-and-twenty, but they changed their minds on getting nearer to him. Old Masey had a way of his own of summing up the peculiarities of his master, repeating twenty times over: 'Sir, he was Strange by name, and Strange by nature, and Strange to look at into the bargain.'

It was during my second or third interview with the old fellow that he uttered the words quoted at the beginning of this plain narrative.

'Not such a thing as a looking-glass in all the house,' the old man said, standing beside my piece of timber, and looking across reflectively at the house opposite. 'Not one.'

'In the sitting-rooms, I suppose you mean?'

'No, sir, I mean sitting-rooms and bedrooms both; there isn't so much as a shaving-glass as big as the palm of your hand anywhere.'

'But how is it?' I asked. 'Why are there no looking-glasses in any of the rooms?'

'Ah, sir!' replied Masey, 'that's what none of us can ever tell. There is the mystery. It's just a fancy on the part of my master. He had some strange fancies, and this was one of them. A pleasant gentleman he was to live with, as any servant could desire. A liberal gentleman, and one who gave but little trouble; always ready with a kind word, and a kind deed, too, for the matter of that. There was not a house in all the parish of St George's (in which we lived before we came down here) where the servants had more holidays or a better table kept; but for all that, he had his queer ways and his fancies, as I may call them, and this was one of them. And the point he made of it, sir,' the old man went on; 'the extent to which that regulation was enforced, whenever a new servant was engaged; and the changes in the establishment it occasioned! In hiring a new servant, the very first stipulation made, was that about the looking-glasses. It was one of my duties to explain the thing, as far as it could be explained, before any servant was taken into the house. "You'll find it an easy place," I used to say, "with a liberal table, good wages, and a deal of leisure; but there's one thing you must make up your mind to; you must do without looking-glasses while you're here, for there isn't one in the house, and, what's more, there never will be."'

'But how did you know there never would be one?' I asked.

'Lor' bless you, sir! If you'd seen and heard all that I'd seen and heard, you could have no doubt about it. Why, only to take one instance:—I remember a particular day when my master had occasion to go into the housekeeper's room, where the cook lived, to see about some alterations that were making, and when a pretty scene took place. The cook—she was a very ugly woman, and awful vain—had left a little bit of a looking-glass, about six inches square, upon the chimney-piece; she had got it surreptitious, and kept it always locked up; but she'd left it out, being called away suddenly, while titivating her hair. I had seen the glass, and was making for the chimney-piece as fast as I could; but master came in front of it before I could get there, and it was all over in a moment. He gave one long piercing look into it, turned deadly pale, and seizing the glass, dashed it into a hundred pieces on the floor, and then stamped upon the fragments and ground them into powder with his feet. He shut himself up for the rest of that day in his own room, first ordering me to discharge the cook, then and there, at a moment's notice.'

'What an extraordinary thing!' I said, pondering.

'Ah, sir,' continued the old man, 'it was astonishing what trouble I had with those women servants. It was difficult to get any that would take the place at all under the circumstances. "What not so much as a mossul to do one's 'air at?" they would say, and they'd go off, in spite of extra wages. Then those who did consent to come, what lies they would tell, to be sure! They would protest that they didn't want to look in the glass, that they never had been in the habit of looking in the glass, and all the while that very wench would have her looking-glass, of some kind or another, hid away among her clothes upstairs. Sooner or later, she would bring it out too, and leave it about somewhere or other (just like the cook), where it was as likely as not that master might see it. And then—for girls like that have no consciences, sir—when I had caught one of 'em at it, she'd turn round as bold as brass, "And how am I to know whether my 'air's parted straight?" she'd say, just as if it hadn't been considered in her wages that that was the very thing which she never was to know while she lived in our house. A vain lot, sir, and the ugly ones always the vainest. There was no end to their dodges. They'd have looking-glasses in the interiors of their workbox-lids, where it was next to impossible that I could find 'em, or inside the covers of hymn-books, or cookery-books, or in their caddies. I recollect one girl, a sly one she was, and marked with the small-pox terrible, who was always reading her prayer-book at odd times. Sometimes I used to think what a religious mind she'd got, and at other times (depending on the mood I was in) I would conclude that it was the marriage service she was studying; but one day, when I got behind her to satisfy my doubts—lo and behold! It was the old story: a bit of glass, without a frame, fastened into the kiver with the outside edges of the sheets of postage-stamps. Dodges! Why they'd keep their looking-glasses in the scullery or the coal-cellar, or leave them in charge of the servants next door, or with the milk-woman round the corner; but have 'em they would. And I don't mind confessing, sir,' said the old man, bringing his long speech to an end, 'that it was an inconveniency not to have so much as a scrap to shave before. I used to go to the barber's at first, but I soon gave that up, and took to wearing my beard as my master did; likewise to keeping my hair'—Mr Masey touched his head as he spoke—'so short, that it didn't require any parting, before or behind.'

I sat for some time lost in amazement, and staring at my companion. My curiosity was powerfully stimulated, and the desire to learn more was very strong within me.

'Had your master any personal defect,' I inquired, 'which might have made it distressing to him to see his own image reflected?'

'By no means, sir,' said the old man. 'He was as handsome a gentleman as you would wish to see: a little delicate-looking and care-worn, perhaps, with a very pale face; but as free from any deformity as you or I, sir. No, sir, no: it was nothing of that.'

'Then what was it? What is it?' I asked desperately. 'Is there no one who is, or has been, in your master's confidence?'

'Yes, sir,' said the old fellow, with his eyes turning to that window opposite. 'There is one person who knows all my master's secrets, and this secret among the rest.'

'And who is that?'

The old man turned round and looked at me fixedly. 'The doctor here,' he said. 'Dr Garden. My master's very old friend.'

'I should like to speak with this gentleman,' I said, involuntarily.

'He is with my master now,' answered Masey. 'He will be coming out presently, and I think I may say he will answer any question you make like to put to him.' As the old man spoke, the door of the house opened, and a middle-aged gentleman, who was tall and thin, but who lost something of his height by a habit of stooping, appeared on the step. Old Masey left me in a moment. He muttered something about taking the doctor's directions, and hastened across the road. The tall gentleman spoke to him for a minute or two very seriously, probably about the patient upstairs, and then it seemed to me from their gestures that I myself was the subject of some further conversation between them. At all events, when old Masey retired into the house, the doctor came across to where I was standing, and addressed me with a very agreeable smile.

'John Masey tells me that you are interested in the case of my poor friend, sir. I am now going back to my house, and if you don't mind the trouble of walking with me, I shall be happy to enlighten you as far as I am able.'

I hastened to make my apologies and express my acknowledgements, and we set off together. When we had reached the doctor's house and were seated in his study, I ventured to inquire after the health of this poor gentleman.

'I am afraid there is no amendment, nor any prospect of amendment,' said the doctor. 'Old Masey has told you something of his strange condition, has he not?'

'Yes, he has told me something,' I answered, 'and he says you know all about it.'

Dr Garden looked very grave. 'I don't know all about it. I only know what happens when he comes into the presence of a looking-glass. But as to the circumstances which have led to his being haunted in the strangest fashion that I ever heard of, I know no more of them than you do.'

'Haunted?' I repeated. 'And in the strangest fashion that you ever heard of?'

Dr Garden smiled at my eagerness, seemed to be collecting his thoughts, and presently went on:

'I made the acquaintance of Mr Oswald Strange in a curious way. It was on board of an Italian steamer, bound from Civita Vecchia to Marseilles. We had been travelling all night. In the morning I was shaving myself in the cabin, when suddenly this man came behind me, glanced for a moment into the small mirror before which I was standing, and then, without a word of warning, tore it from the nail, and dashed it to pieces at my feet. His face was at first livid with passion—it seemed to me rather the passion of fear than of anger—but it changed after a moment, and he seemed ashamed of what he had done. Well,' continued the doctor, relapsing for a moment into a smile, 'of course I was in a devil of a rage. I was operating on my under-jaw, and the start the thing gave me caused me to cut myself. Besides, altogether it seemed an outrageous and insolent thing, and I gave it to poor Strange in a style of language which I am sorry to think of now, but which, I hope, was excusable at the time. As to the offender himself, his confusion and regret, now that his passion was at an end, disarmed me. He sent for the steward, and paid most liberally for the damage done to the steamboat property, explaining to him, and to some other passengers who were present in the cabin, that what had happened had been accidental. For me, however, he had another explanation. Perhaps he felt that I must know it to have been no accident—perhaps he really wished to confide in someone. At all events, he owned to me that what he had done was done under the influence of an uncontrollable impulse—a seizure which took him, he said, at times—something like a fit. He begged my pardon, and entreated that I would endeavour to disassociate him personally from this action, of which he was heartily ashamed. Then he attempted a sickly joke, poor fellow, about his wearing a beard, and feeling a little spiteful, in consequence, when he saw other people taking the trouble to shave; but he said nothing about any infirmity or delusion, and shortly after left me.

'In my professional capacity I could not help taking some interest in Mr Strange. I did not altogether lose sight of him after our sea journey to Marseilles was over. I found him a pleasant companion up to a certain point; but I always felt that there was a reserve about him. He was uncommunicative about his past life, and especially would never allude to anything connected with his travels or his residence in Italy, which, however, I could make out had been a long one. He spoke Italian well, and seemed familiar with the country, but disliked to talk about it.

'During the time we spent together there were seasons when he was so little himself, that I, with a pretty large experience, was almost afraid to be with him. His attacks were violent and sudden in the last degree; and there was one most extraordinary feature connected with them all:— some horrible association of ideas took possession of him whenever he found himself before a looking-glass. And after we had travelled together for a time, I dreaded the sight of a mirror hanging harmlessly against a wall, or a toilet-glass standing on a dressing-table, almost as much as he did.

'Poor Strange was not always affected in the same manner by a looking-glass. Sometimes it seemed to madden him with fury; at other times, it appeared to turn him to stone: remaining motionless and speechless as if attacked by catalepsy. One night—the worst things always happen at night, and oftener than one would think on stormy nights—we arrived at a small town in the central district of Auvergne: a place but little known, out of the line of railways, and to which we had been drawn, partly by the antiquarian attractions which the place possessed, and partly by the beauty of the scenery. The weather had been rather against us. The day had been dull and murky, the heat stifling, and the sky had threatened mischief since the morning. At sundown, these threats were fulfilled. The thunderstorm, which had been all day coming up—as it seemed to us, against the wind—burst over the place where we were lodged, with very great violence.

'There are some practical-minded persons with strong constitutions, who deny roundly that their fellow-creatures are, or can be, affected, in mind or body, by atmospheric influences. I am not a disciple of that school, simply because I cannot believe that those changes of weather, which have so much effect upon animals, and even on inanimate objects, can fail to have some influence on a piece of machinery so sensitive and intricate as the human frame. I think, then, that it was in part owing to the disturbed state of the atmosphere that, on this particular evening I felt nervous and depressed. When my new friend Strange and I parted for the night, I felt as little disposed to go to rest as I ever did in my life. The thunder was still lingering among the mountains in the midst of which our inn was placed. Sometimes it seemed nearer, and at other times further off; but it never left off altogether, except for a few minutes at a time. I was quite unable to shake off a succession of painful ideas which persistently besieged my mind.

'It is hardly necessary to add that I thought from time to time of my travelling-companion in the next room. His image was almost continually before me. He had been dull and depressed all the evening, and when we parted for the night there was a look in his eyes which I could not get out of my memory.

'There was a door between our rooms, and the partition dividing them was not very solid; and yet I had heard no sound since I parted from him which could indicate that he was there at all, much less that he was wide awake and stirring. I was in a mood, sir, which made this silence terrible to me, and so many foolish fancies—as that he was lying there dead, or in a fit, or what not—took possession of me, that at last I could bear it no longer. I went to the door, and, after listening, very attentively but quite in vain, for any sound, I at last knocked pretty sharply. There was no answer. Feeling that longer suspense would be unendurable, I, without more ceremony, turned the handle and went in.

'It was a great bare room, and so imperfectly lighted by a single candle that it was almost impossible—except when the lightning flashed—to see into its great dark corners. A small rickety bedstead stood against one of the walls, shrouded by yellow cotton curtains, passed through a great iron ring in the ceiling. There was, for all other furniture, an old chest-of-drawers which served also as a washing-stand, having a small basin and ewer and a single towel arranged on the top of it. There were, moreover, two ancient chairs and a dressing-table. On this last, stood a large old-fashioned looking-glass with a carved frame.

'I must have seen all these things, because I remember them so well now, but I do not know how I could have seen them, for it seems to me that, from the moment of my entering that room, the action of my senses and of the faculties of my mind was held fast by the ghastly figure which stood motionless before the looking-glass in the middle of the empty room.

'How terrible it was! The weak light of one candle

standing on the table shone upon Strange's face, lighting if from below, and throwing (as I now remember) his shadow, vast and black, upon the wall behind him and upon the ceiling overhead. He was leaning rather forward, with his hands upon the table supporting him, and gazing into the glass which stood before him with a horrible fixity. The sweat on his white face; his rigid features and his pale lips showed in that feeble light were horrible, more than words can tell, to look at. He was so completely stupefied and lost, that the noise I had made in knocking and in entering the room was unobserved by him. Not even when I called him loudly by name did he move or did his face change.

'What a vision of horror that was, in the great dark empty room, in a silence that was something more than negative, that ghastly figure frozen into stone by some unexplained terror! And the silence and the stillness! The very thunder had ceased now. My heart stood still with fear. Then, moved by some instinctive feeling, under whose influence I acted mechanically, I crept with slow steps nearer and nearer to the table, and at last, half expecting to see some spectre even more horrible than this which I saw already, I looked over his shoulder into the looking-glass. I happened to touch his arm, though only in the lightest manner. In that one moment the spell which had held him—who knows how long?—enchained, seemed broken, and he lived in this world again. He turned round upon me, as suddenly as a tiger makes its spring, and seized me by the arm.

'I have told you that even before I entered my friend's room I had felt, all that night, depressed and nervous. The necessity for action at this time was, however, so obvious, and this man's agony made all that I had felt appear so trifling, that much of my own discomfort seemed to leave me. I felt that I must be strong.

'The face before me almost unmanned me. The eyes which looked into mine were so scared with terror, the lips—if I may say so—looked so speechless. The wretched man gazed long into my face and then, still holding me by the arm, slowly, very slowly, turned his head. I had gently tried to move him away from the looking-glass, but he would not stir, and now he was looking into it as fixedly as ever. I could bear this no longer, and, using such force as was necessary, I drew him gradually away, and got him to one of the chairs at the foot of the bed. "Come!" I said—after the long silence my voice, even to myself, sounded strange and hollow—"come! You are over-tired, and you feel the weather. Don't you think you ought to be in bed? Suppose you lie down. Let me try my medical skill in mixing you a composing draught."

'He held my hand, and looked eagerly into my eyes. "I am better now," he said, speaking at last very faintly. Still he looked at me in that wistful way. It seemed as if there were something that he wanted to do or say, but had not sufficient resolution. At length he got up from the chair to which I had led him, and beckoning me to follow him, went across the room to the dressing-table, and stood again before the glass. A violent shudder passed through his frame as he looked into it; but apparently forcing himself to go through with what he had now begun, he remained where he was, and, without looking away, moved to me with his hand to come and stand beside him. I complied.

'"Look in there!" he said, in an almost inaudible tone. He was supported as before, by his hands resting on the table, and could only bow with his head towards the glass to intimate what he meant. "Look in there!" he repeated.

'I did as he asked me.

'"What do you see?" he asked next.

'"See?" I repeated, trying to speak as cheerfully as I could, and describing the reflection of his own face as nearly as I could. "I see a very, very pale face with sunken cheeks—."

'"What?' he cried, with an alarm in his voice which I could not understand.

'"With sunken cheeks," I went on, "and two hollow eyes with large pupils."

'I saw the reflection of my friend's face change, and felt his hand clutch my arm even more tightly than he had done before. I stopped abruptly and looked round at him.

He did not turn his head towards me, but gazing still into the looking-glass, seemed to labour for utterance.

'"What," he stammered at last. "Do - you - see it - too?"

'"See what?" I asked, quickly.

'"That face!" he cried, in accents of horror. "That face—which is not mine—and which—I see instead of mine—always!"

'I was struck speechless by the words. In a moment this mystery was explained—but what an explanation! Worse, a hundred times worse, than anything I had imagined. What! Had this man lost the power of seeing his own image as it was reflected there before him? and, in its place, was there the image of another? He had changed reflections with some other man? The frightfulness of the thought struck me speechless for a time—then I saw how false an impression my silence was conveying.

'"No, no, no!" I cried, as soon as I could speak—"a hundred times, no! I see you, of course, and only you. It was your face I attempted to describe, and no other."

'He seemed not to hear me. "Why, look there!" he said, in a low, indistinct voice, pointing to his own image in the glass. "Whose face do you see there?"

'"Why yours of course." And then, after a moment, I added, "Whose do you see?"

'He answered, like one in a trance, '*His*—only his—always his!" He stood still a moment, and then, with a loud and terrific scream, repeated those words, "ALWAYS HIS, ALWAYS HIS," and fell down in a fit before me.'

'I knew what to do now. Here was a thing at any rate, I could understand. I had with me my usual small stock of medicines and surgical instruments, and I did what was necessary: first to restore my unhappy patient, and next to procure for him the rest he needed so much. He was very ill—at death's door for some days—and I could not leave him, though there was urgent need that I should be back in London. When he began to mend, I sent over to England for my servant—John Masey—whom I knew I could trust. Acquainting him with the outlines of the case,

I left him in charge of my patient, with orders that he should be brought over to this country as soon as he was fit to travel.

'That awful scene was always before me. I saw this devoted man day after day, with the eyes of my imagination, sometimes destroying in his rage the harmless looking-glass, which was the immediate cause of his suffering, sometimes transfixed before the horrid image that turned him to stone. I recollect coming upon him once when we were stopping at a roadside inn, and seeing him stand so by broad daylight. His back turned towards me, and I waited and watched him for nearly half an hour as he stood there motionless and speechless, and appearing not to breathe. This apparition seen so by daylight was more ghastly than the apparition seen in the middle of the night, with the thunder rumbling among the hills.

'Back in London in his own house, where he could command in some sort the objects which should surround him, poor Strange was better than he would have been elsewhere. He seldom went out except at night, but once or twice I have walked with him by daylight, and have seen him terribly agitated when we have had to pass a shop in which looking-glasses were exposed for sale.

'It is nearly a year now since my poor friend followed me down to this place, to which I have retired. For some months he has been daily getting weaker and weaker, and a disease of the lungs has become developed in him, which has brought him to his death-bed. I should add, by-the-way, that John Masey has been his constant companion ever since I brought them together, and I have had, consequently, to look after a new servant.

'And now tell me,' the doctor added, bringing his tale to an end, 'did you ever hear a more miserable history, or was ever man haunted in a more ghastly manner than this man?'

I was about to reply, when we heard a sound of footsteps outside, and before I could speak old Masey entered the room, in haste and disorder.

'I was just telling this gentleman,' the doctor said; not at the moment observing old Masey's changed manner;

'how you deserted me to go over to your present master.'

'Ah! sir,' the man answered, in a troubled voice, 'I'm afraid he won't be my master long.'

The doctor was on his legs in a moment. 'What! Is he worse?'

'I think, sir, he is dying,' said the old man.

'Come with me, sir; you may be of use if you can keep quiet.' The doctor caught up his hat as he addressed me in those words, and in a few minutes we had reached The Compensation House. A few seconds more and we were standing in a darkened room on the first floor, and I saw lying on a bed before me—pale, emaciated and, as it seemed, dying—the man whose story I had just heard.

He was lying with closed eyes when we came into the room, and I had leisure to examine his features. What a tale of misery they told! They were regular and symmetrical in their arrangement, and not without beauty—the beauty of exceeding refinement and delicacy. Force there was none, and perhaps it was to the want of this that the faults—perhaps the crime—which had made the man's life so miserable were to be attributed. Perhaps the crime? Yes, it was not likely that an affliction, lifelong and terrible, such as this he had endured, would come upon him unless some misdeed had provoked the punishment. What misdeed we were soon to know.

It sometimes—I think generally—happens that the presence of anyone who stands and watches beside a sleeping man will wake him, unless his slumbers are unusually heavy. It was so now. While we looked at him, the sleeper awoke very suddenly, and fixed his eyes upon us. He put out his hand and took the doctor's in its feeble grasp. 'Who is that?' he asked next, pointing towards me.

'Do you wish him to go? The gentleman knows something of your sufferings, and is powerfully interested in your case; but he will leave us, if you wish it,' the doctor said.

'No. Let him stay.'

Seating myself out of sight, but where I could both see and hear what passed, I waited for what should follow. Dr Garden and John Masey stood beside the bed. There was a moment's pause.

'I want a looking-glass,' said Strange, without a word of preface.

We all started to hear him say those words.

'I am dying,' said Strange; 'will you not grant me my request?'

Dr Garden whispered to old Masey; and the latter left the room. He was not absent long, having gone no further than the next house. He held an oval-framed mirror in his hand when he returned. A shudder passed through the body of the sick man as he saw it.

'Put it down' he said, faintly—'anywhere—for the present.' Not one of us spoke. I do not think, in that moment of suspense, that we could, any of us, have spoken if we had tried.

The sick man tried to raise himself a little. 'Prop me up,' he said. 'I speak with difficulty—I have something to say.'

They put pillows behind him, so as to raise his head and body.

'I have presently a use for it,' he said, indicating the mirror. 'I want to see —' He stopped, and seemed to change his mind. He was sparing of his words. 'I want to tell you—all about it.' Again he was silent. Then he seemed to make a great effort, and spoke once more, beginning very abruptly.

'I loved my wife fondly. I loved her—her name was Lucy. She was English; but, after we were married, we lived long abroad—in Italy. She liked the country, and I liked what she liked. She liked to draw, too, and I got her a master. He was an Italian. I will not give his name. We always called him "the Master". A treacherous insidious man this was, and, under cover of his profession, took advantage of his opportunities, and taught my wife to love him—to love him.

'I am short of breath. I need not enter into details as to how I found them out; but I did find them out. We were away on a sketching expedition when I made my discovery. My rage maddened me, and there was one at hand who fomented my madness. My wife had a maid, who, it seemed, had also loved this man—the Master—and had

108

been ill-treated and deserted by him. She told me all. She had played the part of go-between—had carried letters. When she told me these things, it was night, in a solitary Italian town, among the mountains. "He is in his room now," she said, "writing to her."

'A frenzy took possession of me as I listened to those words. I am naturally vindictive—remember that—and now my longing for revenge was like a thirst. Travelling in those lonely regions, I was armed, and when the woman said, "He is writing to your wife," I laid hold of my pistols, as by an instinct. It has been some comfort to me since, that I took them both. Perhaps, at that moment, I may have meant fairly by him—meant that we should fight. I don't know what I meant, quite. The woman's words, "He is in his own room now, writing to her," rung in my ears.'

The sick man stopped to take a breath. It seemed an hour, though it was probably not more than two minutes, before he spoke again.

'I managed to get into his room unobserved. Indeed, he was altogether absorbed in what he was doing. He was sitting at the only table in the room, writing at a travelling-desk, by the light of a single candle. It was a rude dressing-table, and—and before him—exactly before him—there was—there was a looking-glass.

'I stole up behind him as he sat and wrote by the light of the candle. I looked over his shoulder at the letter, and I read, "Dearest Lucy, my love, my darling." As I read the words, I pulled the trigger of the pistol I held in my right hand, and killed him—killed him—but, before he died, he looked up once—not at me, but at my image before him in the glass, and his face—such a face—has been there—ever since, and mine—my face—is gone!'

He fell back exhausted, and we all pressed forward thinking that he must be dead, he lay so still.

But he had not yet passed away. He revived under the influence of stimulants. He tried to speak, and muttered indistinctly from time to time words of which we could sometimes make no sense. We understood, however, that he had been tried by an Italian tribunal, and had been found guilty; but with such extenuating circumstances that his sentence was commuted to imprisonment, during, we thought we made out, two years. But we could not understand what he said about his wife, though we gathered that she was still alive, from something he whispered to the doctor of there being provision made for her in his will.

He lay in a doze for something more than an hour after he had told his tale, and then he woke up quite suddenly, as he had done when we had first entered the room. He looked round uneasily in all directions, until his eye fell on the looking-glass.

'I want it,' he said, hastily; but I noticed that he did not shudder now as it was brought near. When old Masey approached, holding it in his hand, and crying like a child, Dr Garden came forward and stood between him and his master, taking the hand of poor Strange in his.

'Is this wise?' he asked. 'Is it good, do you think, to revive this misery of your life now, when it is so near its close? The chastisement of your crime,' he added, solemnly, 'has been a terrible one. Let us hope in God's mercy that your punishment is over.'

The dying man raised himself with a last great effort, and looked up at the doctor with such an expression on his face as none of us had seen on any face, before.

'I do hope so,' he said, faintly, 'but you must let me have my way in this—for if, now, when I look, I see aright—once more—I shall then hope yet more strongly—for I shall take it as a sign.'

The doctor stood aside without another word, when he heard the dying man speak thus, and the old servant drew near, and, stooping over softly, held the looking-glass before his master. Presently afterwards, we, who stood around looking breathlessly at him, saw such a rapture upon his face, as left no doubt upon our minds that the face which had haunted him so long, had, in his last hour, disappeared.

ALL CHANGE

John Edgell

Have you ever stood in an Underground station at midnight—alone? The eight-car platform seems to be as large as a cathedral and a cold wind sighs eerily from the gaping mouths of the tunnels. In the distance you can hear a weird wail that, if you are brave enough to investigate, you will find emanates from the rubber hand-rails of the escalators as they rub ceaselessly.

The first passenger cars of the City and South London Railway came to be known as 'the padded cells'. They had no windows (except for ventilation slits high above the backs of the seats) and the passenger seats faced inward because the builders believed that there was nothing to see in a tunnel. In 1890 the conductor announced the names of the stations. An example of a 'padded cell' can be seen today, exhibited at the Railway Museum, York.

The reality is intimidating enough; but to the nervous, and especially to the imaginative schoolboy, the Underground can be a fearsome place.

IT WAS GETTING late. Tammy hurried to the Underground station and bought his ticket. When he had telephoned his aunt an hour and a half before, she had said the bed would be ready for him, so long as he did not arrive too late. He mustn't expect her to stay up until all hours. If he didn't arrive by midnight she would assume that he wasn't coming.

Tammy mixed with the noisy theatre and cinema crowds on the platform, and pushed his way towards the large indicator which swung high above. There were so many names on it, that he could not be sure which train to catch.

He stopped a guard on the platform.

'Which train should I catch for Potter's End?' he said.

'Ah, Potter's End.' The guard peered at him. 'Potter's End, yes. Well, take the third train on the indicator, you see it up there? The third train will take you to Potter's End.' The guard turned away into the crowds, and Tammy waited at the edge of the platform.

He saw the lights of the next train approaching from inside the tunnel. The whole station began to shake and echo with the noise, and he forced his way back a few steps from the edge as the train pushed in. He did not like crowds.

The doors of the train opened, and many of the people clambered aboard, pushing and shouting; a crowd of drunks at the end of the platform were quarrelling about which train to catch. In the end some of them got on the train, and the others didn't.

'Mind the doors, mind the doors!' shouted the guard

over everyone's heads. the electric doors drew together, and the train began to accelerate rapidly out of the station, until only its red tail light glowed in the blackness of the tunnel.

Few people were left on the platform. An engaged couple strolled slowly up and down, and stopped to laugh at a cinema poster. Their voices echoed strangely under the round ceiling. A man in an old overcoat fought with a chocolate machine, pulling and tugging on the tray to get the chocolate. A sixpence fell on the floor.

After a moment, the indicator began to flash again, and the numbers changed. Tammy knew that the train he wanted now was number two, not number three. The train that had been number two before now became number one. People began edging towards the front of the platform.

A slow growl gradually filled Tammy's ears, and the next train burst into the station, filling it with a screeching noise as all the doors slid open. All the way along the platform Tammy could see people getting off the train, and everyone else struggling past to climb aboard it.

'Any more for any more!' shouted the guard. 'Mind the doors!' The doors of the train closed, and slowly the train began to move out of the station. Tammy tried to watch each carriage as it passed, but they passed so quickly that he could not keep turning his head fast enough. Then, with a muffled echo, the last carriage plunged into the black tunnel, and the vibrations came to a stop.

The platform was empty; scraps of paper blew about. It was a long time before anything happened. The indicator seemed quiet for several minutes, before the numbers and the letters began to flash again. The train on the indicator which had been the second train before now became the first train, and Tammy knew that this was the train that had been the third train when he had asked for the one to Potter's End. The indicator made Tammy feel rather muddled, but he had counted two trains so far, which meant that his train would be the next one. The station was growing unpleasantly dim.

He heard the echo of the guard's footsteps as the guard

paced slowly up and down the empty station. A very old woman came down the stairs and began to sweep the platform with a long broom. Tammy felt very cold inside.

He did not have a watch, but when he looked up at the cracked station clock he began to feel sure it had stopped. Or was it just his imagination?—he could not be sure. But at a guess, it had stopped for at least seven or eight minutes. He tried staring at the hands of the clock without blinking, to see if he could notice the minute hand moving. But then he blinked, and could not be sure that the hands hadn't moved.

Then the guard looked up. The old woman leaned on her broom. The vibrations began to shake the station, and in a minute Tammy could see the lights of the train curving in the tunnel towards them. Then, like an explosion, the train hurtled into the station. Tammy stepped forward. It seemed to be going very fast. Could it stop in time? Tammy watched anxiously. He was frightened to see that none of the lights were on in the train. All the carriages which raced past were dark and empty. The station reverberated with the sound of the train clicking over the track, until in a flash it was swallowed in the tunnel.

The guard looked up at him.

'Going to the depot,' he said.

Tammy sat down on a bench and waited. Waiting made him feel nervous, so he felt in his pocket for a sixpence to buy some chocolate. He put the sixpence in the machine, and heard it fall down the slot. But all the trays were stuck. He had lost his sixpence, and he hadn't had any chocolate. He looked round to tell the guard.

But the guard had vanished, and so had the woman with the broom.

Tammy looked at the indicator. There was just one train listed, number one. Tammy wondered why more trains hadn't been indicated, as when he had first reached the platform with all the theatre crowds. He wondered if all those people had got home safely. Then he thought, it is late, perhaps this is the last train. Was he the only person going to catch it? He was certain the station clock had stopped now.

He must have been standing around for at least eleven or twelve minutes since he had last looked at it. He shivered. The clock was old, it needed someone to repair it. It glowered down from its iron cradle.

Then Tammy heard the train. A slow and distant rumble echoed in the tunnel, and made the railway lines shake. At last, Tammy saw the lights at the front of the train, and the train itself entered the station. Tammy stepped back from the edge of the platform. The train came to a halt; at least the lights were on in the carriages. The doors slid open.

'Last train!' said the guard. Tammy looked round, but neither the guard nor the old woman were anywhere to be seen. Tammy began to feel scared.

The carriage was a non-smoker. Tammy went in, and sat down right at the very end, on one of those folding seats that come out from the wall. The doors closed. Slowly, the train began to move out of the station, and as Tammy looked out of the window, all he could see was a garish blur of colours. Then they roared into the tunnel, and he could see the neat row of electric cables dancing past in the side of the tunnel. Suddenly, the cables seemed to lift slightly, and then plunge down below the level of the window.

Tammy was alone in the carriage. Looking through the windows, he saw that all the other carriages were empty, too. He wondered how far it was to Potter's End. Would his aunt still be waiting up for him? Then, as he was sitting on the folding seat, he heard the creak of a door handle turning behind him.

Tammy had never seen anyone walk from one carriage to another. the doors usually remained closed. But someone was trying to move into his carriage from the next one. What could they want? Tammy began to rise from his seat, and the seat suddenly slammed shut. He jumped. He could see no one through the window on the other side. All he could see was rows and rows of empty seats: it was like looking into a hall of mirrors. And yet—someone, or something, was there.

When the door opened wide, Tammy saw the guard who had been on the platform—but the guard was dead. Towards the terrified boy came a skeleton of grey discoloured bones. Over the skull was the peaked cap; over the shoulder blades and ribs, the official coat and jacket hung like loose skin. As the skeleton approached, its bones knocked softly together. The jaw of the skull was fixed in an unnatural grin. Behind it came the dead woman who had been sweeping the platform, still clutching her broom.

Tammy backed away down the other end of the carriage, but he moved in slow motion, as if in a dream. His legs and arms would not do what his brain wanted; he swam helplessly in the heavy air, screaming as he fought to drag one leaden foot behind the other.

Out of the corner of his eye, he felt the train coming slowly and irresistibly to a halt. He had just struggled to the far end of the carriage with his back against the wall, when the doors slid open several yards wide. Out of the blackness moved a solemn procession of seven undertakers with black hats and capes, bearing a small wooden coffin.

Screaming and screaming, Tammy stretched out his hands to protect himself. The arms which slid from his jacket sleeves were the bones of a skeleton.

The guard stood, a sentinel of death, at the side of the seven undertakers.

'All change,' he said.

MIDNIGHT EXPRESS

A. Noyes

Books serve many purposes. They inform and inspire and, in the case of steam-railways, are becoming almost the only source of information. In their turn they have inspired many young engineers and have provided the enthusiasm that is expressed in the opening of abandoned railway-lines by amateurs.

Macabre stories, hopefully, inspire pleasurable thrills of horror, although, as has has been demonstrated in these pages, they are at their best when they are rooted in mundane, if historically romantic, fact. The solidarity of the subject gives realism to the supernatural aspects of the story and enhances their impact.

In Midnight Express an illustration in a book inspires fear and when the contents of the page are translated into fact the usual process is not reversed but heightened and fear is heaped upon fear. The plot is unusually complex for a writer of the Victorian Era and for so short a story, which makes it a rarity. The editor hopes that it will not only give the reader pleasure, but cause him to consider the power, and dangers, of books.

IT WAS A battered old book, bound in red buckram. He found it, when he was twelve years old, on an upper shelf in his father's library; and, against all the rules, he took it to his bedroom to read by candlelight, when the rest of the rambling old Elizabethan house was flooded with darkness. That was how young Mortimer always thought of it. His own room was a little isolated cell, in which, with stolen candle ends, he could keep the surrounding darkness at bay, while everyone else had surrendered to sleep and allowed the outer night to come flooding in. By contrast with those unconscious ones, his elders, it made him feel intensely alive in every nerve and fibre of his young brain. The ticking of the grandfather clock in the hall below, the beating of his own heart; the long-drawn rhythmical 'ah' of the sea on the distant coast, all filled him with a sense of overwhelming mystery; and, as he read, the soft thud of a blinded moth, striking the wall above the candle, would make him start and listen like a creature of the woods at the sound of a cracking twig.

The battered old book had the strangest fascination for him, though he never quite grasped the thread of the story. It was called *The Midnight Express*, and there was one illustration, on the fiftieth page, at which he could never bear to look. It frightened him.

Young Mortimer never understood the effect of that picture on him. He was an imaginative, but not a neurotic youngster; and he avoided the fiftieth page as he might have hurried past a dark corner on the stairs when he was six years old, or as the grown man on the lonely road, in *The Ancient Mariner*, who, having once looked round, walks on, and turns no more his head. There was nothing in the picture—apparently—to account for this haunting dread. Darkness, indeed, was almost its chief characteristic. It showed an empty railway platform—at night—lit by a single dreary lamp: an empty railway platform that suggested a deserted and lonely junction in some remote part of the country. There was only one figure on the platform: the dark figure of a man, standing almost directly under the lamp with his face turned away towards the black mouth of a tunnel which—for some strange reason—plunged the imagination of the child into a pit of horror. The man seemed to be listening. His attitude was tense, expectant, as though he were awaiting some fearful tragedy. There was nothing in the text, so far as the child read, and could understand, to account for this waking nightmare. He could neither resist the fascination of the book, nor face that picture in the stillness and loneliness of the night. He pinned it down to the page facing it with two long pins, so that he should not come upon it by accident. Then he determined to read the whole story through. But, always, before he came to page fifty, he fell asleep; and the outlines of what he had read were blurred; and the next night he had to begin again; and again, before he came to the fiftieth page, he fell asleep.

He grew up, and forgot all about the book and the picture. But halfway through his life at that strange and critical time when Dante entered the dark wood, leaving the direct path behind him, he found himself, a little before midnight, waiting for a train at a lonely junction; and, as the station-clock began to strike twelve, he remembered; remembered like a man awakening from a long dream—.

There, under the single dreary lamp, on the long glimmering platform, was the dark and solitary figure that he knew. Its face was turned away from him towards the black mouth of the tunnel. It seemed to be listening, tense, expectant, just as it had been thirty-eight years ago.

But he was not frightened now, as he had been in childhood. He would go up to that solitary figure, confront it, and see the face that had so long been hidden,

122

so long averted from him. He would walk up quietly, and make some excuse for speaking to it: he would ask it, for instance, if the train was going to be late. It should be easy for a grown man to do this; but his hands were clenched, when he took the first step, as if he, too, were tense and expectant. Quietly, but with the old vague instincts awaking, he went towards the dark figure under the lamp, passed it, swung round abuptly to speak to it; and saw— without speaking, without being able to speak —.

It was himself—staring back at himself—as in some mocking mirror, his own eyes alive in his own white face, looking into his own eyes, alive —.

The nerves of his heart tingled as though their own electric currents would paralyse it. A wave of panic went through him. He turned, gasped, stumbled, broke into a blind run, out through the deserted and echoing ticket-office, on to the long moonlit road behind the station. The whole countryside seemed to be utterly deserted. The moonbeams flooded it with the loneliness of their own deserted satellite.

He paused for a moment, and heard, like the echo of his own footsteps, the stumbling run of something that followed over the wooden floor within the ticket-office. Then he abandoned himself shamelessly to his fear; and ran, sweating like a terrified beast, down the long white road between the two endless lines of ghostly poplars each answering another, into what seemed an infinite distance. On one side of the road there was a long straight canal, in which one of the lines of poplars was again endlessly reflected. He heard the footsteps echoing behind him. They seemed to be slowly, but steadily, gaining upon him. A quarter of a mile away, he saw a small white cottage by the roadside, a white cottage with two dark windows and door that somehow suggested a human face. He thought to himself that, if he could reach it in time, he might find shelter and security—escape.

The thin implacable footsteps, echoing his own, were still some way off when he lurched, gasping, into the little porch; rattled the latch, thrust at the door, and found it locked against him. There was no bell or knocker. He pounded on the wood with his fists until his knuckles .bled. The response was horribly slow. At last, he heard heavier footsteps within the cottage. Slowly they descended the creaking stair. Slowly the door was unlocked. A tall shadowy figure stood before him, holding a lighted candle, in such a way that he could see little either of the holder's face or form; but to his dumb horror there seemed to be a cerecloth wrapped round the face.

No words passed between them. The figure beckoned him in; and, as he obeyed, it locked the door behind him. Then, beckoning him again, without a word, the figure went before him up the crooked stair, with the ghostly candle casting huge and grotesque shadows on the whitewashed walls and ceiling.

They entered an upper room, in which there was a bright fire burning, with an armchair on either side of it, and a small oak table, on which there lay a battered old book, bound in dark red buckram. It seemed as though the guest had been long expected and all things were prepared.

The figure pointed to one of the armchairs, placed the candlestick on the table by the book (for there was no other light but that of the fire) and withdrew without a word, locking the door behind him.

Mortimer looked at the candlestick. It seemed familiar. The smell of the guttering wax brought back the little room in the old Elizabethan house. He picked up the book with trembling fingers. He recognised it at once, though he had long forgotten everything about the story. He remembered the ink stain on the title page; and then, with a shock of recollection, he came on the fiftieth page, which he had pinned down in childhood. The pins were still there. He touched them again—the very pins which his trembling fingers had used so long ago.

He turned back to the beginning. He was determined to read it to the end now, and discover what it all was about. He felt that it must all be set down there, in print; and, though in childhood he could not understand it, he would be able to fathom it now.

It was called *The Midnight Express*; and, as he read the

first paragraph, it began to dawn upon him slowly, fearfully, inevitably.

It was the story of a man who, in childhood, long ago, had chanced upon a book, in which there was a picture that frightened him. He had grown up and forgotten it and one night, upon a lonely railway platform, he had found himself in the remembered scene of the picture; he had confronted the solitary figure under the lamp; recognised it, and fled in panic. He had taken shelter in a wayside cottage; had been led to an upper room, found the book awaiting him and had begun to read it right through, to the very end, at last—. And this book, too, was called The Midnight Express. *And it was the story of a man who, in childhood—. It would go on thus, forever and forever, and forever. There was no escape.*

But when the story came to the wayside cottage, for the third time, a deeper suspicion began to dawn upon him, slowly, fearfully, inevitably—. Although there was no escape, he could at least try to grasp more clearly the details of the strange circle, the fearful wheel, in which he was moving.

There was nothing new about the details. They had been there all the time; but he had not grasped their significance. That was all. *The strange and dreadful being that had led him up the crooked stair—who and what was That?*

The story mentioned something that had escaped him. The strange host, who had given him shelter, was about his own height. Could it be that he also—and was this why the face was hidden?

At the very moment when he asked himself that question, he heard the click of the key in the locked door.

The strange host was entering—moving towards him from behind—casting a grotesque shadow, larger than human, on the white walls in the guttering candlelight.

It was there, seated on the other side of the fire, facing him. With a horrible nonchalance, as a woman might prepare to remove a veil, it raised its hands to unwind the cerecloth from its face. He knew to whom it would belong. But would it be dead or living?

There was no way out but one. As Mortimer plunged forward and seized the tormentor by the throat, his own throat was gripped with the same brutal force. The echoes of their strangled cry were indistinguishable; and when the last confused sounds died out together, the stillness of the room was so deep that you might have heard—the ticking of the old grandfather clock, and the long-drawn rhythmical 'ah' of the sea, on a distant coast, thirty-eight years ago.

But Mortimer had escaped at last. Perhaps, after all he had caught the midnight express.

It was a battered old book, bound in red buckram....

THE LAST TRAIN

Harry Harrison

The Underground station in war-time lost its appearance of desolation. To escape the air-raids and flying bombs, people flocked to the protection of the Underground to sleep safely at night; lying upon the platform in rows. They were convivial, sometimes even gay, and there was no room in their minds for ghosts or other horrors. But horror did come, as you will see; for this story is based upon fact.

Although the popularity of the macabre story was on the decline between the wars and was much neglected by authors, a new theme had been developed that stemmed from the same advances in science and technology that was increasing the popularity of Science Fiction. This theme was based upon the proposition that if the 'ghost' of a person or thing from the past is seen, in some way it might be possible that they had been displaced in the dimension of time for a short period. This offered an alternative scientific explanation to the usual 'spirit' explanation while being equally mysterious.

This theme saw many variations; but possibly this subtle blending of fact and fiction by Harry Harrison is the best example of all.

'LOOK, IT'S BEEN one of those days, not to mention one of those nights before. I have a chill I can't lose. Do you think I could have a double whisky, or even a treble.'

'Treble. Of course.' I signalled the barman. George Wolsey is an enthusiastic American most of the time, but when he is low he is very low. 'Too much drink? Chill on the liver?'

'No, neither of those. You wouldn't believe me if I told you.'

'My gullibility is beyond comprehension.'

'Maybe. But this is one of those things that people are sure to laugh at.'

'Should I laugh?'

'No way. This is serious, dead serious—though I shouldn't use that word. Dead, I mean.'

He gulped his drink with more rush than pleasure, and I wondered just what was troubling him. A solid head on even more solid shoulders. Been in government for more years than I care to remember, visited all of the outlandish parts of the world on his country's business. Someone I could never imagine being in a panic—yet here he was now, pallid of skin and drinking good Glenlivet in a disgraceful manner.

'Do tell me,' I said. 'I take it to be a serious matter and have no intention of laughing. I have a cigar and a drink and you have my utmost attention.'

George cracked his knuckles and stared deeply into his glass.

'Maybe you should laugh. Maybe I drank too much and was squiffed out of my mind. I don't know. Maybe you can tell me. It was late last night, early this morning really, just after twelve midnight. There were old friends, the usual thing, drink flowing like water, an overheated room, and I was tired from the day. It was in a flat in Ashburn Gardens, just off the Cromwell Road. Drank too much, not alone in that as you can well imagine, and when I finally looked at my watch I couldn't believe it. Me with one of those damned seven-thirty breakfasts in the morning. I said I was going to the loo, that's the only way to get away from these parties, grabbed my coat and was out of the door without anyone knowing it. The air felt good and I started to walk, then realised that I was going the wrong way. No cabs this time of night in Kensington, and if there were any they would probably be at the air terminal. I was on the Gloucester Road, I didn't feel like turning back—and there was the tube entrance in front of me.'

He scooped peanuts out of the dish on the bar and ate the entire handful at once, chewing at them ferociously as though it were his last supper. I said nothing but aspirated a smoke ring as comment and, in a moment, he continued.

'I knew the station well enough, had used it often thirty-odd years ago when State had this top-secret office right around the corner. Fine bit of Victorian railway architecture that station—did you ever notice it? District and Circle Lines, name right up there in eternal ceramic tile. First underground in London. Not really underground, surface cut, coal engines and all that.'

He sipped his drink again and it was obvious even to himself that he was avoiding the real topic, for his knuckles were white where he held the glass. Finally he 'bit the bullet', in his favourite American idiom, and squared his shoulders.

'My hotel's right on the Circle Line, the gate was open, the last train usually runs a bit past midnight so I should have been able to grab it. And I could hear a rumble and felt a bit of breeze in my face. Down the steps I went, two at a time, digging five pence out of my pocket as I went so I could buy a ticket. The stairwell was dark and a little grim, nothing unusual there as you well know, and it continued right down to the platform. No ticket machines or anyone in sight. I must have gone down an exit by mistake. They open and shut things differently late at night. Anyway, I came to the bottom and there, just ahead, was the train with the doors standing open. A shilling saved, I remember thinking that, then tottering forward as fast as I could and through the doors which shut right behind me. I stood there, breathing heavily, waiting for the train to move. It didn't. That was the first thing.'

George stared into his glass for a very long time, almost as though he had forgotten my presence.

'The first thing?' I asked, as quietly as I could.

He shook himself and spoke again, in a voice so low I had to strain to hear it.

'The first thing wrong. Why wasn't the train moving? No crowds or waiting for other trains at that time of night. Yet we just stood there and stood there and I looked around and felt this sudden, penetrating chill. The heat in the car was turned off, saving energy, I remember thinking that, yet it was more than a physical chill. That's the only way to describe it, something that went through my entire body in a second. My feet inside my shoes felt frozen, every inch of my skin recoiled from the same cold bite. I hugged my arms about myself and wondered if I wasn't coming down with something. Yet everyone else in the car was well bundled up, so maybe it wasn't just me. It was pretty crowded for that time of night. The last train can be. Just the usual crowd of people, some sitting, some standing. Heavy coats, wool scarves, old macs—and all of them absolutely silent under the dim yellow light bulbs.

'Then, I swear it, I was sober in an instant. Not that I had been drunk before, nothing like that. Just plenty of good booze, fatigue, relaxed, ready for bed. Then it was gone. I was chill and I was sober and I could feel the hair crawl on the back of my neck just as though I had been dropped into a pit brimming with vipers. It is what I had seen. This is the time when you mustn't laugh.'

I said nothing. He wasn't even looking at me but staring

131

ahead, wide-eyed, seeing something visible only to himself.

'It was a paper, just that, a newspaper, jammed into a man's shabby raincoat pocket. A morning paper, *The Times*, thin and flimsy. When I glanced down it wasn't two feet from my face and I could see the name and read the date quite clearly. 8 December, 1941. Now don't say anything.'

I had no intention, of course.

'It could have been an old newspaper, why not? A souvenir or something. What does a single old paper mean? Very little by itself. But it was the people as well. They were shabby, I mean real war-time shabby, with the well used and patched clothing, the pale grey skins of war-time rations, that look of fatigue that we all seemed to feel most of the time. It wasn't just one thing, it wasn't anything specific—or maybe a lot of small things. I can't put a name to it but I do know that all of a sudden, in that chill and unmoving train, surrounded by those silent drab people, I felt fear. Fear of a kind that I have never felt before, and you know what I mean when I say that, what with Yugoslavia and the entire Mediterranean thing. I have been afraid—who hasn't?—but this was the kind of fear that is a single hairbreadth away from death itself. I felt that if I remained there an instant longer I *would* be dead. Without any thought or control I turned and clawed at the closed doors. Clawed. I've heard that word before, very popular in a certain kind of novel as you know, but I *did* it. I tore at those doors, clawed them, did this in an instant.

He held up his right hand and, for the first time, I felt some of the very chill he had been talking about.

For every nail on his hand was broken right down into the quick, torn away, black with clotted blood and iodine. I realised then he had been holding his glass in his left hand, his right in his jacket pocket all the time.

'It was panic, sheer panic, for of course the doors did not open. I looked over my shoulder and became aware that the people in the car were turning to look at me. Their backs were all turned and now, slowly, all their heads were moving as one. And I did not want to see their faces. God, I didn't.

'How long this moment lasted I cannot tell you. An instant or a thousand years. It went on and on and on and the heads kept turning my way and the chill was in my bones and I felt the solid world of life crumbling from beneath my feet and the emptiness of death and eternity opening up under me.

'But it was the doors that opened instead. I was pressing so solidly back against them that I shot out onto the platform, staggering and falling. You know how the doors in tube trains sometimes open and shut for an instant. Well this was what happened. They did it just that quickly and if I hadn't dropped back that way I wouldn't have got out. The doors instantly slammed shut again like steel jaws and the train began to move. I just stayed there, on my hands and knees, and watched it rumble the length of the platform and into the tunnel beyond, its lights getting yellower then dimmer. And then it was gone. I pulled myself up and had to hold to the wall so I shouldn't fall again. Then there was a rattle of gates and a man, a guard, was calling to me angrily. The station was closed, last train gone, I shouldn't be there—the righteous anger of minor authority abused. I mumbled something and went out through the gate he held open for me, clashing it emphatically behind me, and climbed back to the Gloucester Road, just in time to wave down a passing cab. And that is it. I suppose. Not something one should get upset about?'

It was phrased as a question and was a difficult one to answer. I covered the moment by ordering a round of drinks and collected my thoughts a bit before I spoke.

'I wouldn't say that. You *were* upset, so there had to be a reason. I imagine all of the bits can be explained, separate explanations, just that, but when they came together they did not have the world's most beneficial effect upon you. . . .'

George smiled in a most understanding manner; if I had been a dog he would have patted my head. I shut up.

'I should tell you one thing more,' he said. 'The date on

133

the newspaper is one I shall never forget, because it is one that brought the terror of the war closest to me. On 8 December 1941 there was a last train from Gloucester Road. Filled with tired people, exhausted people yearning to be home and warm and asleep. When the train left the station it went into that bit of tunnel then out again into the open cutting before the Kensington High Street station. What happened next was one of the most horrifying and unforeseen circumstances. There was no raid on. Yet a bomb was dropped. Perhaps a German pilot on his way home letting a last one drop at random. A land mine. One of the really big ones. It dropped into that cutting and exploded on the train and one hundred and twelve people were dead on the instant. Living people suddenly just mangled bits of flesh and bone.'

At that George fell silent and I did too. We do tend to forget how bad things were and it is not pleasant to be reminded. I finally coughed a bit and spoke.

'Yes, of course, I can see how you felt. This train, years later, reminded you of an earlier train. Perfectly comprehensible.'

'No, it is not. You still do not understand completely. You see, on that other December night I missed the train, a train that I took every single night. I arrived just that little bit late and actually pulled at the doors, but they would not open. I watched it leave and I was angry and was still standing there when the explosion came, lighting up the sky like a view of hell, blowing me from my feet.

'I missed that train. But, tell me, has it been waiting for me all those years? Always there on this day at this hour. Should I have been aboard it with the others?

'Then, if I *had* taken it last night, what would have happened to me?'

THE TALE OF A GAS-LIGHT GHOST

Anonymous

There was a deplorable aspect to the growth of the British Railway System. This was the unplanned proliferation of comparatively short railways financed by groups of businessmen who knew they could realise a profit by moving their own and other people's goods. Sometimes they built rival lines almost side-by-side, as in the case of the Liverpool to Manchester lines that became so vital to the cotton trade.

It was necessary for these Company promoters to ask Parliament to pass a Bill to enable them to acquisition the land upon which the railway was to be built. Not all land-owners and small farmers wanted to part with their lands and numerous law-suits resulted. Joseph Locke, in his presidential address to the Institution of Civil Engineers, condemned this system and declared that in most cases a quarter of the capital subscribed by the shareholders was spent in getting the Bill through Parliament. Sometimes opposition came from the canal owners who were now losing freighting contracts to the railways and their power can be seen at such towns as Buxton and Hemel Hempstead where the railway station is some distance from the town centre.

In the year 1845 Parliament authorised the building of 2,170 miles of railways and by the early part of the following year was considering 477 more Bills. Many of these schemes came to nothing, dishonest company promoters had a field-day and modest speculators lost their life-savings.

The following story, written within a decade of these events, tells of a group of local land-owners banding together to oppose a proposed railway. Perhaps they should have been more cautious about who they admitted into their ranks.

'Tis an easy thing for me to tell you a story of ghosts, for from my childhood I have been accustomed to hear of them; from my infancy I was taught to believe in them. Not the old nurses' tales of white-draped spectres, of grinning skulls and ghastly goblins; but the well-authenticated appearances after death of those known upon earth, in the dress they wore when toiling in the world.

Ghosts ran in the Dale family, people said jeeringly— insanity too, they added; and from time to time we have been made the butts for jokes of those would-be wags, who refuse to believe anything which does not happen to have come under their own narrow experience. I could tell you a story of my great-grandfather, who was haunted by the spirit of a man he slew in a duel, who followed him in spirit form wherever he went, beckoning to him from the midst of a crowd at times; at others visiting him in the solitude of his chamber, till my great-grandfather, driven to frenzy, one day drew his sword and nearly ran his butler through the body for denying the ghost of the murdered man stood by him. The constant terror of this continual appearance drove my ancestor out of his mind though, of course, there were people who declared he was out of his mind in the first instance.

So of Roderick Dale, his son, who was haunted by an unknown figure, and finished his days in a lunatic asylum; so of Charles Mervyn, his nephew, who was again and again surprised by the apparition of his father, starting as it were from out the wall upon him. I could tell you all these stories, but you would not even pretend to listen to them.

The story I am about to tell you is quite different from these. It happened less than two years ago. There are a dozen men alive at the present day to vouch for its truth; and it does not depend on any of the usual ghost properties for its effect. In it there is no dismal ruined mansion, no desolate churchyard, no bell tolling the hour of midnight, no rattling of chains or hollow groanings; in short, it is a matter-of-fact ghost story, with none of the ordinary paraphernalia generally supposed to appertain to the spirit world. In order, however, that you may understand it properly, I must give you a short description of the parish of Mapleton, and a few of its inhabitants some twenty months since.

Mapleton is an essentially agricultural parish; its acreage is large, and so are its tillers; its population is small, and so are its wants; its politics are conservative, its society is exclusive, and its ignorance of the other parts of the world is great. Furthermore, its landowners are few and wealthy, and its tenant-farmers well-to-do and contented. It was on record that only one farmer had ever been dissatisfied with the state of things at Mapleton—a young man who had considered the old house in which generations of his ancestors had been born and died too gloomy for him, and had built himself a brand new house of a mixture of the cottage and villa style, on the outskirts of the village, and had immediately gone to the dogs, and had been forced to seek a living away from his native place.

Thus it came about that there was a house to let in Mapleton; but how Gregory Barnstake came to know of it, and how, knowing it, he came to take it, after it had remained empty several years, was never understood. Where he came from nobody knew—who he was no one could find out. He was a severely handsome man, by which I mean that his face in marble would have been called superb, but in flesh and blood it was too hard and too expressionless; he was neither young nor old; he had no friends who came to see him, and he appeared to be well off. Society at Mapleton settled that from such a man it would be well to keep aloof until something was known

138

of his antecedents, but Gregory Barnstake never gave society an opportunity of showing its feelings, for he avoided as much as possible even necessary intercourse with his neighbours, and, as the villagers put it, 'kept himself to himself'.

The doctor was the only man in the parish who had ever entered his house. Gregory Barnstake one afternoon fell down in a fit and his servant ran to Dr Sweetman and brought him in all haste to where the new inhabitant of Mapleton lay stretched on a couch with his limbs cold and stiff and his eyes fixed and glassy, looking more like a corpse than a man.

In an hour's time the rigidity left his limbs, and his eyes assumed their ordinary expression. Sitting up, his glance rested somewhat angrily on the doctor.

'Who are you?' he asked abruptly.

'Doctor Sweetman. I heard from your servant that you were ill, and came to see if I could be of service.'

'Thank you. When I want physic I will send for you.'

The doctor, who was as merry and good-natured a little round man as you could wish to meet with, took this, of course, as a dismissal, and not a very polite one. He was not prone to take offence, but he could not feel very pleased with such a reception.

'Good day, sir,' he said, opening the door.

'Stay a moment, doctor, I beg,' said Mr Barnstake, 'I fear I have offended you. Let me explain to you that these fits of mine come upon me at intervals. I can never tell when to expect them. They seize me and leave me in a state of torpor for one, two, or sometimes three hours, during which time no doctor's skill could benefit me. When they have passed, I recover at once, as you see I have done now.'

'Is your mind unconscious at the time?' asked Dr Sweetman.

'Unconscious of the present, but living in the past,' was the answer with a weary sigh.

'Have you any pain when you are attacked in the first instance?'

'Yes. I feel as if a hand of ice were laid over my heart;

then that its hold tightens, causing me exquisite pain, till at last I fall senseless.'

'Hum!' said the doctor, 'a curious but not an unprecedented case. If you would allow me to send you something I fancy I could alleviate your sufferings.'

'Quite a mistake. You doctors go on prescribing medicine till you believe in their efficacy.'

'You have a bad opinion of the profession,' responded the doctor.

'Not of the profession so much, perhaps, as of those who practise it. The world is composed of knaves and fools; the fools take the medicines, the knaves prescribe.'

Retorted the doctor hotly:

'Then, sir, I am to conclude that you alone are superior to the world at large, as you are neither knave enough to prescribe, nor fool enough to take, prescriptions.'

'You are to conclude nothing of the sort, but to see in me an unfortunate man whose love of playing the knave led him on to play the fool, and reduced him to what he now is. If you knew the story of my life you—.'

'Well, sir?'

'You would know the story of a miserable man.'

The doctor had to be content with that ending to the sentence, and took his leave, puzzling his head to make out whether he had been talking to a man whose brains were a little touched, or whether his conversation had been with one of those dark and mysterious heroes so often met with in books and melodramas, but so seldom in real life.

The months went by at Mapleton, the crops were gathered in and sown again, and Gregory Barnstake remained as great a mystery as ever. With the doctor he had had on one or two occasions short conversations, but with no one else had he interchanged more than a few words of abrupt courtesy.

A time came, however, when he was driven to consort with his neighbours. An enterprising railway company, having discovered there was no iron-road near Mapleton, sent out its staff of surveyors to walk over the farms and inspect the country, with a view to making a branch line from Overbury through Mapleton to Harstone Heath, and the landowners rose in a body to repel the intrusive steam engines.

Gregory Barnstake received a letter to inform him of these facts, and that a meeting, commencing with a dinner, was to be held at the 'Seven Stars' on a certain day for the purpose of remonstrating, petitioning, and doing anything that might be necessary to stop the proposed railway. To this letter he returned no answer.

A second was sent, repeating the substance of the first and adding the information that his house was the proposed site of the station. To this he rejoined that he was sorry to hear it, as he should certainly leave the place in the event of a railroad coming there, but that at the same time he must decline to attend the dinner.

However, still further pressure was put upon him, till at last, in an interview with Dr Sweetman, he said angrily:

'Well, well, to save further words I will attend, but bear in mind whatever may happen I am not responsible.'

There were many reasons why his presence was so much desired at the meeting, the principal being that he was a person much interested, as the whole of the land he held on lease would be required by the railway company. Another, that it was whispered that he was very clever; that he read Latin and Greek books for amusement; and that mysterious volumes of matter incomprehensible, save to the learned, lay generally on the table by his side. Now the Mapletonians, as a rule, knew more of farming than of literature, and it was deemed that to have a man amongst them who would polish up any petition they might send forward, and to see the correctness of expression in such letters as they might consider it incumbent on them to write, would be of the greatest advantage; and so it was that Gregory Barnstake was worried into a reluctant assent to attend the meeting.

The day, big with fate for the Mapletonians, arrived. The landowners and the majority of tenant-farmers met in the largest room of the 'Seven Stars', and, punctual to the minute, Gregory Barnstake entered. As the door opened to give him admission, he happened to be the subject of the conversation, and an awkward silence ensued as he came forward; but one or two speedily advanced towards him and gave him a hearty welcome, thanking him for breaking through his rule of never mixing with his neighbours, and hoping that, now he had commenced, they might often have the pleasure of seeing him, to all of which he answered gravely and seriously, that it was no pleasure to him to mix in what was called society; but, as they had pressed him so much to be present on this occasion, he had felt he must do as they desired, 'but,' he added, speaking loudly enough for the whole room to hear, 'in accepting your invitation, I omitted to state that it would be impossible for me to come alone, and, therefore, I must beg that a chair may be set apart for another guest.'

Everyone was astonished, for never had Gregory Barnstake been seen talking familiarly with anyone, never had he been supposed to have any intimate; and yet there was someone from whom he could not be separated himself even for a few hours.

'Is your friend in any way interested in this proposed railway encroachment?' asked the squire.

'Not in the least.'

'Has he any property about here?'

'None whatever.'

'We have not expected anyone here today,' stammered the squire, getting very red in the face, 'who was not in some way connected or, at all events, interested in the subject we have met to discuss, but, of course—.'

'If you have any objection I will at once withdraw.'

'No, no; on no account. I was about to add that any friend of yours we would accept.'

There was a silence, then a short desultory conversation, and in the middle of it dinner was announced.

'Has your friend arrived?' asked the squire of his strange acquaintance. 'I see no unfamiliar face amongst us.'

'He is not here, yet, but he is sure to come. If I may keep this seat next to me vacant for him, it is all I require.'

No objection was made, the party took their seats, leaving that one chair unoccupied; the covers were removed, and the dinner commenced.

There was not much conversation then, for the Maple-tonians held that to dine was one of the chief duties of man; but ere the first course was at an end the entire party, with one accord, raised their eyes from their plates and fixed them on a figure sitting in the chair that had been left vacant. Gregory Barnstake alone seemed quiet and unsurprised. In the chair by his side sat a man, remarkable more for his aristocratic appearance than for any beauty of feature. His age, apparently, was between forty and fifty; his hair and whiskers were iron grey, and arranged with scrupulous neatness and precision; but the most extraordinary thing about him was his complexion, which was of a pale ash hue, such as to cause more than one to shudder and wonder. Another peculiarity about him was his attire. He was in full evening dress. His black coat and spotless shirt front, his sparkling studs and snowy cravat, contrasted strangely with the farmers' shooting jackets and the squire's bird's-eye neckerchief.

Quietly he sat at the table, eating nothing, but trifling with the fork that lay beside his plate. No one had seen him enter, no one had observed him take his seat, but there he sat as calmly and unconcernedly as if he were a bidden guest, known to the whole company.

As he played with the fork with his left hand another fact was apparent, which was that the second and third fingers on that hand were wanting.

It was strange that, while the whole table paused to regard the stranger the only person who seemed uncon-scious of his presence was he who sat by his side, and through whose agency he was in the room. There was a great awkwardness about it, the squire thought, for Gregory Barnstake had apparently no intention of intro-ducing him, and not one of the company seated in that warm gas-lighted room, with a good dinner on the table before them, but felt a sensation of uneasiness, for which they were totally unable to account.

'Come, gentlemen,' said the squire, feeling it incumbent upon some one to break the silence, 'there's no occasion for so much solemnity, I hope. Mr Parkhurst, pleasure of a glass of wine with you?'

Mr Parkhurst filled his glass.

'Ah,' continued the squire, 'I remember old Tony buying this wine—very good it is too—let me see when it was; '44, I think.'

'No,' said the stranger, ''48.'

'I beg your pardon sir. Did you know Tony Bean?'

The stranger shook his head.

'Anyhow it was in the year Jem Hales was transported for poaching. His time's up now; he'll be coming home soon, I suppose.'

'Jem Hales will never come home,' said the stranger.

'Do you know him then?'

'I saw him a short time since.'

'Indeed. In England?'

'No.'

'Where is he now?'

'In his grave.'

The squire gazed, not without a certain amount of fear, on the uninvited guest, and pursued the matter no further.

The conversation at the dinner-table languished, and, in spite of one or two attempts to revive it, it finally died into confidential whisperings between those sitting next each other.

With the removal of the cloth the spirits of the company revived, and the squire getting on his legs, inveighed with all the eloquence of which he was master against all the railway companies, and that one in particular which threatened to destroy the primitive innocence of Mapleton. Everybody spoke at once, and the meeting had like to have proved a failure, but Gregory Barnstake, rousing himself, made a speech such as had never been heard in Mapleton, putting all the facts before them clearly and concisely, and urging the immediate drawing up and signing of the proposed petition.

All this time the stranger sat calm and immovable, but when preparations were being made for framing the petition he spoke.

'You may spare yourself the trouble,' he said; 'your

144

petition will be of no avail.'

'How do you know that?' asked the squire sharply.

'I state a fact.'

'Perhaps you are a shareholder in the company,' said a farmer, in a tone meant to be sarcastic.

'This day nineteen months,' said the stranger, 'a train will pass through Mapleton.'

'I hope you are a false prophet, sir,' said the squire.

'I am not,' rejoined the other.

In spite of his prediction, the petition was drawn up and signed, and the meeting broke up.

'You see we persevere in our plan, although you predict failure,' said the squire, putting on his hat.

The stranger bowed.

'Good evening, sir.'

'We shall meet again. In eight weeks.'

'You are certainly a very circumstantial prophet,' answered the squire, and with a slight bow he left the room.

Said Dr Sweetman, taking Gregory Barnstake by the button, 'An extraordinary-looking man, your friend.'

'Very.'

'Excuse me, I don't wish to be impertinent, but, in the interest of my profession, do you know if he is suffering from any internal disease?'

'He is not. I can answer for it,' said Gregory with a slight shudder.

'It is strange. I never saw a living man with such a complexion.'

'He is not a living man,' was the reply, and the speaker walked away, leaving the little doctor gazing after him in frightened astonishment.

Eight weeks after this dinner the squire was out with the hounds, and his horse, in taking a hedge, stumbled, and pitched his rider over his head. The squire was not hurt, neither was the horse, for he trotted away, leaving his owner to follow as best he might, and over the fields and hedges he went, till, on emerging from a small copse, he saw his steed standing by a pond, and near to him the figure of a man. The man was dressed in spotless evening attire, and was without a hat and the squire in a moment identified him as the stranger at the dinner two months before.

His appearance had been singular enough within the walls of the 'Seven Stars', but now to meet him in a precisely similar dress in the open country was much more startling, and the squire, though a brave man, would have avoided him if possible; he would have given a well-filled purse to have been able to reach his horse without passing by the motionless figure, but it was an impossibility, so, raising his hat and putting as bold a face on it as he could, he thanked the stranger for catching his beast, but received not a syllable in response. Only, at last, when he had remounted his horse did the figure move, then it turned towards him, and, stretching out the hand on which the two fingers were missing, pointed to the water.

The squire set spurs to his horse and rode away.

The days became weeks, and the weeks months, the railway company got permission to make their line through Mapleton, and some hundred navvies were busily employed in making an embankment. In draining the pond which was memorable to the squire they found something which induced them to leave off work for the time, and send for the authorities to the spot, and that something was the skeleton of a man half-buried in the mud.

Dr Sweetman was, of course, amongst those summoned. The bones were left untouched for his inspection.

'It's strange,' he said, when he had finished his inspection, 'but there are two fingers wanting.'

There was nothing to be done after the inquiry but to place the bones in a coffin and inter them in the churchyard; but an idea had come into the doctor's head—a fancy—that Gregory Barnstake might know something of the skeleton. Had not that mysterious friend of his lacked two fingers of his left hand? So the doctor, on his way home, called at the house at the end of the village.

He rapped at the door with his knuckles, but received no answer. The door was on the latch and he pushed it open. He entered the sitting room where he had had his first interview with its strange occupant, and the first thing that met his eyes was Gregory Barnstake stretched on the floor, his handsome face terribly distorted with pain—dead!

Was he really dead, or was it only one of those strange fits to which he was subject. The little doctor tried every test, and decided it was really death that had come upon him; that the agony of one of those fits had killed him. For the rest, I hardly dare tell you; but nevertheless it is true that, when the body came to be examined, over the heart were distinctly discernible the livid marks as of a hand pressed tightly there, but of a hand of which the second and third fingers were wanting.

That is the story I had to tell you. You are welcome to put what interpretation on it you please. It was a mystery, and a mystery it will always remain. I cannot attempt to give you a clue to one of the strangest stories it has ever been my lot to hear and know to be true.

In conclusion, I can only add that there are now at least a dozen men alive who can vouch for the accuracy of the facts I have stated, but who, like myself, whatever may be their opinions, forbear to attempt an explanation of this strange occurrence to which I, perhaps without sufficient reason, have given the name of 'The Tale of a Gas-light Ghost'.

THE ATTIC EXPRESS

Alex Hamilton

Model trains have evolved in their own way. From the first crude, wooden models carved by railway workers for their children, the art has grown into an industry so that rolling-stock made with the precision of a Swiss watch are now available. Miniaturisation has made it possible for the civil engineering aspects of the model railway to be elaborately reproduced in a modest space with a great deal of realism.

The old joke about the father who plays with his son's model railway no longer applies. There is no place for a child on a real model lay-out and a father who involves his son against his will is courting disaster for he will find himself facing the very real and primitive power of hatred. Children are primitives, and magical laws often govern their outlook and behaviour; and when pre-adolescent malignity is at its strongest only evil can ensue.

This was the force behind many historical cases of possession, of poltergeists and the Salem Witch Trials. In The Attic Express Alex Hamilton combines these two themes and takes them to the ultimate.

IN THE EVENINGS they climbed the steep narrow stairway to the big room under the roof. Hector Coley went up eagerly and alertly. The boy followed his father draggingly. In the family it had always been called 'Brian's room', but to Brian it seemed that his father's presence filled it.

It was a long room, with low side-walls and a ceiling like the lower half of an A. There was a large water-tank at one end: the rest of the space was 'Brian's'.

Coley ran the trains. The boy looked on.

Sometimes, when his father was absorbed, attending to midget couplings, rearranging a length of track, wiring up a tiny house so that it could be lit from inside, he looked away, and merely watched the single square of attic window gently darken.

Coley hated Brian to lose interest. He would say irritably: 'I can't understand you, Brian, beggared if I can. You know something? Some boys would give an arm to have the run of a play-room like this one I've built for you.'

The boy would shift his gaze and rub his hands together nervously. He would stoop forward hastily and peer at all parts of the track. 'Make it go through the crossing,' he would say, to appease his father. But even before the magnificent little Fleischmann engine challenged the gradient to the crossing—which would involve the delicious manoeuvre of braking two or three small cars—his eye would be away again, after a moth on the wall, or a cloud veiling the moon.

'It defeats me,' Coley would say later to his wife, 'he shows no interest in anything. Sometimes I don't get a

151

word out of him all evening unless I drag it out of him.'

'Perhaps he's not old enough yet,' she would reply diffidently. 'You know, I think I'd find it a little difficult to manage myself—all those signals and control switches and lights going on and off and the trains going this way and that way. I'm glad I'm never asked to work out anything more complicated than a Fair Isle knitting pattern.'

'You miss the point,' said Coley impatiently. 'I'm not expecting him to synchronise the running times of ten trains, and keep them all safely on the move, but I would like a spark of enthusiasm to show now and again. I mean, I give up hours of my time, not to speak of money running into thousands, to give him a lay-out which I'm willing to wager a couple of bob can't be matched in any home in Britain, and he can't even do me the courtesy of listening to me when I explain something. It's not good enough.'

'I know, dear, how you feel, but at ten I do feel it's a little—.'

'Oh, rubbish,' exclaimed Coley, 'ten's a helluvan age. At ten I could dismantle a good watch and put it together again better than new.'

'You are exceptional, dear. Not everyone has your mechanical bent. I expect Brian's will show itself in time.'

'There again, will it? His reports all read the same: "Could do much better if he applied himself more ... doesn't get his teeth into it ..." and so on till I could give him a jolly good hiding. No, Meg, say what you like, it's plain to me that the boy won't try.'

'In some subjects he's probably a little better than in others.'

'Nonsense,' said Coley energetically, 'anybody can do anything, if they want to enough.'

One evening, after listening to his complaints meekly for a while, she suddenly interrupted him:

'Where is he now?'

'Where I left him. I've given him the new express in its box. I want to see whether he's got enough gumption to set it out on the track with the right load. If I find it's still in the box when I get back—.'

'Yes, dear,' she said, surprising him with her ve-hemence, 'why don't you bring the matter to a head? It's getting on my nerves a bit, you know, to be down here reading and watching television, and to imagine you struggling. If he's not really interested, then could we have an end to all this? I know the railways are your pride, but honestly I'd rather see them scrapped than listen to any more of this.'

He was astonished. He went back upstairs without a word.

The boy was squatting, with his face cupped in one hand, elbow on knee. His straight brown hair fell forward and half obscured his face. The other arm dangled loosely, and the forefinger of his hand moved an empty truck to and fro a few inches on the floor.

The express was on the rails, Brian had it at the head of an extraordinary miscellaneous collection of waggons: Pullmans, goods trucks, restaurant cars, breakdown wag-gons, timber trucks, oil canisters—anything, obviously, which had come to hand.

'Sit down at the control panel, Brian,' snapped Coley.

The boy did not reply, but he did what he was told.

'I want you to run this express tonight,' said Coley, 'and I'm not going to lift a finger to help. But I'll be fair, too, I won't criticise. I'll stay right out of it. In fact for all you know I might as well be on the train itself. Think of me being on it, that's it, and run it accordingly. . . .'

He was trying to keep the anger and disappointment out of his voice. The boy half turned a moment, and looked at him steadily, then he resumed his scrutiny of the control panel.

'. . . take your time . . . think it all out . . . don't do anything hastily . . . keep your wits about you . . . remem-ber all I've taught you . . . that's a gorgeous little model I've got there for you . . . I'm on board . . . up on the footplate if you like . . . we'll have a gala and just have it lit with the illuminations of the set itself . . . give me time to get aboard . . . I'm in your hands, son. . . .'

Coley stood on the main line. The giant express faced him, quiet, just off the main line. He started to walk along the track towards it.

He felt no astonishment at finding himself in scale with the models. *Anyone can do anything, if they want to enough.* He'd wished to drive a model, from the footplate, and here he was walking towards it.

But at the first step he took he sank almost up to his knees in the ballast below the track. It was, after all, only foam rubber. He grinned. 'I'll have to remember things like that,' he told himself.

He stopped by the engine and looked up at the boiler. He whistled softly between his teeth, excited by so much beauty. What a lovely job these Germans made of anything they tackled. Not a plate out of line. A really sumptuous, genuine, top-of-the-form job. He wished the maker a ton of good dinners. The thing was real, not a doubt.

He stepped on through tiny, incisive pebbles of sand, treading cautiously. One or two had threatened to cut into his shoes. Looking down, he noticed a right-angled bar of metal, gleaming at his feet. He realised in a moment that it must be one of the staples which had held the engine's box together. Chuckling over his own drollness at playing the game to the full, he picked up the bar and with an effort almost succeeded in straightening it right out. Then he advanced on the wheel and tapped it. The wheel was, of course, sound. He ran his hand over the virgin wheel. He lifted his arm and placed his hand against the smooth gloss of the boiler. He could do that because it was quite cold. He smiled again: that took away a bit of the realism, to think of a steam engine run on electricity. When you were down to scale it seemed you noticed these things.

Then he frowned as he noticed something else. The coupling of the first carriage, a Pullman, could not have been properly made up by Brian. The first wheels were well clear of the rails. He ran past the tender to have a look. Sure enough. Damn careless of him. He was about to call out to Brian when he remembered his promise to say nothing, and thought he'd make the correction himself. It was just a matter of sliding the arm across until the spoke fell into the slot in the rear of the tender. The remainder of the fastening was simple. He jabbed the lever in under the arm and strained to shift the carriage.

After a minute, during which the carriage swayed a bit but did not move, he stopped and took off his coat. He was still in his office suit. He wished he were in his old flannels and lumberjack shirt, but at least he hadn't changed into slippers. Sweat trickled down his back. He hadn't had much time for exercise lately, though his usual practice was conditioning on the links, alternate fifteen yards running and walking, for eighteen holes. Without clubs of course.

He hurled himself at it again, bracing his full weight against the lever. Suddenly the arm shifted, and skidded over the new surface on which it rested. The spoke found the slot, and the whole carriage crashed into position on the rails. The lever flicked off with rending force, and one spinning end struck him under the arm, just near the shoulder.

He thought he would be sick with pain. All feeling went out of his arm, except at the point of impact. There was plenty of feeling, all vividly unpleasant. Almost mechanically he leant down and picked up his jacket. Trailing it, he tottered back to the engine, and slowly hoisted himself into the cab. There he leant over one of the immobile levers until he had partially recovered.

He was still palpating his startled flesh, and established that no bone was broken, when, without any preliminary warning, the train suddenly jerked into motion. Wheeling round, he managed to save himself from falling by hooking himself into the window of the cab. He looked for his son, to signal he was not quite ready yet. Even without the blow he had just sustained he would have liked a few more minutes to adjust himself to the idea of being part of a model world before the journey began.

But he couldn't at first see where he was. In this fantastic landscape, lit but not warmed by three suns, all the familiar features had undergone a change. The sensation resembled in some way that which comes to a man who visits a district he knows well by daylight for the first time after dark.

In the direct light of those three suns, an overhead monster and two wall brackets, everything glittered. Plain to Coley, but less noticeable to the boy at the table on which was spread the control panel, were separate shadows of differing intensity radiating from every upright object. But the objects themselves sparkled. Light came flashing and twinkling and glancing from the walls and roofs of the houses, from the foliage of the trees, from the heaps of coal by the sidings, from the clothes and faces of the men and women. The lines of the railway themselves shone, twisting and turning a hundred times amongst windmills and farms and garages and fields and stations, all throwing back this aggressive, stupefying brilliance of light. Coley screwed up his eyes and tried to work it out. The train slipped forward smoothly, gaining momentum. The boy hadn't made a bad job of the start, anyway. Perhaps he took in more than I imagined, said Coley to himself.

He fixed his eye on a vast grey expanse, stretching away parallel to the course they were on, and appearing like a long rectangular field of some kind of close undergrowth with curling tops. What the devil could that be? He didn't remember putting down anything like that. Whatever it was, it didn't look anything like the real thing, now that he was down to scale. A breeze stirred small clumps which seemed to ride clear of the rest, and it came to him that, of course, this was the strip of carpet he'd laid down on one side of the room, always insisting that people should walk only on this if possible, to prevent breakages.

If that was the carpet ... he rushed across to the other window, just in time before the engine started to take a corner to see the top of his son's head, bent over the controls.

It was miles away. So huge. So ... dare he admit it to himself ... grotesque. The line of his parting, running white across his scalp, showed to the man in the cab like a streak in a forest, a blaze consequent upon road-making. A house could have been hidden behind the hair falling across his forehead. The shadow of his son on the burning white sky behind was like a stormcloud.

Brian disappeared from his view as the track curled, and Coley shook his head, as if he could clear away these images as a dog rattles away drops of water from its fur. 'It's not like me to imagine things,' said Coley fiercely. All the same, beads of moisture stood out on the back of the hand which clutched a lever.

He sensed a slight acceleration. The telegraph poles were coming by now at more than one a second. He felt the use of his injured arm returning, and with it a return of self-confidence. 'I wonder if, when I return to my normal size, the bruise will be to scale or be only, quite literally, a scratch?'

He was about to resume his jacket, since the wind was now considerable, when the train turned again and he lost his balance. In falling, the jacket fell from his hand, and was whipped away out of the cab.

Unhurt by his fall, but irritated by the loss of the jacket, Coley pulled himself to his feet and swore: 'Hell of a lot of bends on this railway,' as if he were perceiving it for the first time. 'Anyway, that doesn't matter so much, I can put up with a fresh wind for a while if he'd only think what all this bloody light is doing to my eyes. Tone down the ruddy glare, can't you?'

As if in answer, the suns were extinguished.

For an instant the succeeding blackness was complete.

The express forged almost noiselessly through the dark. Coley fumbled for handholds. 'That's a bit inefficient,' he muttered. But the totality of darkness was not for long. Simultaneously, and Coley imagined Brian studying the switches, all the lights in the houses and stations and farms and windmills, and so forth, were flipped on.

'That's really rather nice to look at,' said Coley, appreciatively. 'I always knew I'd done a good job there, but it's only now that I can see just how good. I don't think they can complain there,' he went on. 'I think they'd admit I've looked after that little creature comfort.' He was referring to the little people with whom he had populated the world in which the attic express was running.

He also thought, as the walls of the attic vanished altogether: 'If he hasn't noticed that the old man's no longer sitting in the armchair behind him he's not likely to now. It would be rather good to slip back into the chair before the lights go up again. I'll have to watch my moment as soon as he's had enough and stops the express.'

They sped through a crossing. Coley, looking down on it and at the figures massed by the gate, observed a solitary figure in a patch of light, waving. Whimsically, he waved back. The expression on the face of the waving man was one of jubilation. His smile reached, literally, from ear to ear. 'A cheery chappie,' remarked Coley. He was beginning to enjoy himself.

At a comfortable pace the express swung into a long straight which led into the area described on the posters and signboards as Coleyville. It was the largest and best equipped of the five stations. Coley thought that Brian must see it as an inevitable stop. Interesting to see whether he could bring it in to a nice easy check. The passengers might be assumed to be taking down their suitcases, and dragging on their coats, and would be resentful at being overbalanced.

Far up ahead Coley could see the platform approaching. He could make out the long line of people waiting to climb aboard. A representative body of folk, thought Coley, I got in a good cross section of the travelling public for Coleyville. Then, flashing down the hill, on the road which would cross the track just this side of the station in a scissors intersection, Coley saw an open sports car. It was coming down at a frightening speed, and should reach the junction just as the express went through.

'The young monkey,' breathed Coley, 'he must be getting into the swing of it.' For a moment he tensed, until he remembered that on this crossing there was a synchronisation which would automatically brake the car. A high, whining metallic noise filled his ears from the single rail of the roadster, which abruptly cut off as the car was stopped.

'From eighty to rest in a split second,' thought Coley, 'that's not too realistic. Not the boy's fault, but I'll have to see if I can't improve on that.' He also noticed, as the express moved slowly through the crossing, that there were no features on the face of the roadster's driver. Not even eyes. 'No use telling you to look where you're going,' shouted Coley. The square-shouldered driver sat upright and motionless, waiting for the express to be out of his way.

The express stopped at Coleyville.

'Perfect,' exclaimed Coley, 'just perfect.' He wished he could shake Brian's hand. The boy must care, after all, to be able to handle the stuff in this way. His heart swelled. He thought for a moment of stepping off at Coleyville and watching from the outside for a while, and then pick her up again next time she stopped. But he couldn't be sure the boy would bring her round again on the same line. And this was far too exhilarating an adventure to duck out now. He stayed.

He leant out of the cab and looked down the platform at the people waiting. It was a mild surprise to him that no one moved. There they stood, their baggage in their hands or at their feet, waiting for trains, and doing nothing about it when one came. He saw the guard, staring at him. The guard's face was a violent maroon colour, and the front part of one foot was missing. He had doubtless good reasons for drinking heavily. Immediately behind him was a lovely blonde, about seven feet high, and with one breast considerably larger than the other, but otherwise delicious to look at. At her side was a small boy in suit and school cap. He had the face of a middle-aged man. Farther on down, a toothless mastiff gambolled, at the end of a leash held by a gentleman in city suit and homburg. He was flawless but for the fact that he had omitted to put on collar and tie.

Coley rubbed the side of his nose with his index finger. 'I never expected to discover that you had such curious characters,' he said ruefully. The guard stared at him balefully, the blonde proudly. The express moved out of the station. Coley took his shoe off and hammered the glass out of the right-hand foreport. It was too opaque for proper vision. He smiled as he thought of the faces of the makers if he should write to them criticising. Being

Germans, they'd take it seriously, and put the matter right in future.

Beyond Coleyville the track wound through low hills. Coleyville was a dormitory town, but on the outskirts were some prosperous farms whose flocks could be seen all about the hills. A well-appointed country club lay at the foot of the high land which bordered the east wall, which was continued in illusion by a massive photograph of the Pennines which Coley had blown up to extend most of the length of the wall. It was, in Coley's view, one of the most agreeable and meticulously arranged districts in his entire layout.

By the fences of the farms stood children, waving. Yokels waved. Lambs and dogs frisked. A water-mill turned slowly. It ran on a battery, but looked very real. Plump milkmaids meandered to and fro. 'Lovely spot for a holiday,' thought urban Coley, sentimentally. He leant far out of the cab window to have a better view of the whole wide perspective, and almost had his head taken off by a passing goods train.

It came up very softly, passing on the outside of a curve. Coley withdrew his head only because he happened to catch a slight shadow approach.

He leant his face against the cold metal by his window. 'Idiot,' he said to himself in fright and anger.

The goods train went by at a smart clip. There were only about five trucks on it, all empty.

'Steady, old chap' he apostrophised his son, under his breath, 'don't take on too much all at once.'

For the first time it occurred to him that it might be a good thing to be ready to skip clear in the event of danger. Brian was operating very sensibly at present, but a lapse in concentration ... a vague chill passed down Coley's spine.

He looked back at the train on which he was travelling. It might be better to pick his way to the rear coaches.

He took three strides and launched himself onto the tender. Landing, he tore his trousers on the rough surface which represented coal nuts. It was very slippery and he almost slid right over it altogether, but he contrived to dig toes and hands into the depressions and check himself.

The express was moving along an embankment. Below him he could see the figures of young women in bathing suits disporting themselves about a glass swimming pool. Uniformed waiters stood obsequiously about, handing drinks to shirt-sleeved gentlemen under beach umbrellas. In the context of night-time the scene appeared macabre and hinting of recondite pleasures, particularly when the white legs of one of the beauties, protruding from under a glistering, russet bush, were taken into account. She could have been a corpse, and none of the high-lifers caring.

Coley wriggled forward cautiously over the hard black lumps. He wished now he'd stayed where he was, since the strong wind was more than he had allowed for.

He scrambled to a sitting position on the hard, pointed surface of the tender. Beyond the country club, looking ahead, were the mountains. He sought about for the secure footholds he'd need before making his leap off the tender into the gaping doorway of the Pullman behind, but decided to postpone the effort until the express had passed through the long tunnel. There was a long gentle declivity on the far side, a gradient of 1:248—he'd posted it—and he'd have a more stable vehicle to jump to. Besides, in the tunnel it would be dark.

He remembered himself one Sunday morning making the mountain secure above the tunnel. The trouble he'd had with that material, nailing it in firmly without damaging any of the features of the landscape built on to it.

Those nails.

Some must protrude into the tunnel itself. He'd never troubled himself about them. There had always been plenty of clearance for the trains themselves. But for him, perched on top of the tender? He looked round desperately to see if he might still have time to make his leap.

But he remembered too late. The tunnel sucked them in like a mouth. He rolled flat on his face and prayed.

It was not completely dark, though very nearly so. A vague glow came through at one section where a tricky bit of building had been finally effected with painted canvas, and in it he was lucky to spot one of the nails and wriggle clear. The other he never saw. The point, aimed perpendicularly downwards, just caught his collar, as it arched upward over his straining neck.

He was jerked up bodily. It was very swift. He had no time to do anything about it. For a second he seemed to be suspended on the very tip of the nail, then the shirt tore and he was delivered back on the train.

He landed with a vicious thump on some part of a waggon some distance below roof-level. Something drove like the tip of a boot into his knee and he doubled over against what might be a rail. He clung to it. He couldn't tell where he was, but he could hear a wheel clicking furiously beneath him. Gasping from the pain of his knee, and a dull throb between the shoulder blades he hung on and waited for the end of the tunnel and light.

It came suddenly.

His first feeling was relief that he had been thrown almost on the very spot he had chosen to jump to before the train entered the tunnel. But this was succeeded by a stab of anguish from his back as he raised himself to his feet in the doorway of the Pullman. He put his hand behind his back and found first that his shirt had split all the way to his trousers. He allowed it to flow down his arms, and held it in one hand while he probed his back with the other.

'Ye gods,' he murmured shakily, as he examined his hand after feeling his wound, 'I must be bleeding like a stuck pig.'

Slowly he converted his shirt into a great bandage, wrapping it around his chest, under his armpits, and tying it below his chin, like a bra in reverse. While he was doing this, grunting as much from astonishment at his predicament as from pain, the express accelerated, and as it thundered along the decline his horror at this was added to the confusion of his feelings.

'I must stop this,' he said thickly. 'I must signal the boy to cut the power off.' He reeled into the Pullman. On the far side he seemed to remember there was a flat truck with nothing on it but a couple of logs. Perhaps if he got astride

162

one of them he could make himself be seen.

From nowhere appeared the colossal torso of a man. It was white-coated, but the face was mottled, a sort of piebald, with only one deeply sunken eye, and the other the faintest smear at the point of the normal cheekbone.

'Get away. Get away,' screamed Coley, striking out at it wildly. One of the blows landed high on the man's chest. He teetered a moment, and then, without bending, went over on his back. The material from which he was made was very light. He was no more than an amalgam of plastics and painted hat.

Coley looked down at the prostrate dummy and rubbed his bloodied hand over his forehead. 'No sense in getting hysterial,' he warned himself. He stepped over the prostrate figure, twisting to avoid the outstretched arm. He observed with revulsion that the fingers on the hand were webbed, a glittering duck-egg blue. Coley ran his tongue over his lips, tasting blood. 'Take a brace,' he admonished himself, reverting to the slang of his schooldays, 'don't let your imagination run away with you.'

He staggered amongst the conclaves of seated gentlemen, for ever impassive and at their ease in armchairs, content with the society in which they found themselves, unimpressed by the increasing momentum of the express, welded to their very chairs. Coley shot a glance over the gleaming carapace of one stern hock-drinker and out through the window. The variety of the landscape was flickering by with alarming speed, becoming a gale of altering colours. The coach was beginning to sway.

Coley broke into a run. The roar below him apprised him that the express was travelling over the suspension bridge. The bridge had been his pride, a labour of months, not bought whole, but built from wire and plywood in his leisure hours. He had no time now for gloating.

'I must get him to see me or I'm done for.'

But beyond the Pullman he found another waggon, a restaurant car. In his haste he had forgotten that one. He dashed down the aisle, grabbing tables to steady himself against the rocking of the train as he went. They must be up to seventy now. Or rather about four miles an hour, he realised with bitterness.

Leaning a moment over one of the tables, he saw that the lamps in the centre were bulky, heavy-looking objects. He heaved tentatively at one of them, and it snapped off at the base. The diners, with their hands in their laps, stared on across the table at each other, untroubled by the onslaught of this wild-eyed Englishman. The Englishman, naked to the waist, his shirt sleeves dangling red and filthy down his chest, his body flaming now with a dozen bruises, stood over them a second clutching the lamp to him, panting heavily, then turned away and reeled on down the aisle. Down his retreating back the blood was flowing now freely. The shirt was inadequate to check it as it escaped from the savage wound he had sustained in the tunnel.

This time when he emerged at the doorway of the carriage he found himself looking at the open truck on which were chained four logs. He flung the lampstand ahead of him and it landed satisfyingly between two of the logs. He gathered his ebbing strength for the jump.

He was just able to make it. He caught his foot in one of the chains in mid-flight and crashed down on his face, but he saved himself from disaster by flinging one arm round a log. He sat up immediately and looked about him.

For a moment his vision was partly blocked as yet another train flashed by in the opposite direction. 'Oh God, what's he playing at?' whispered Coley, 'he can't handle so many trains at once.'

The express was almost at the end of the long straight. It slowed for the curve right, at the bottom. For a brief time after that it would be running directly under the control panel at which Brian was sitting. That would be his chance to make an impression. He hauled himself astride the top log and waited.

The express took the curve at a reduced pace, but squealing slightly nevertheless. Coley could sense most of the load concentrate on the inner wheels. Then he could see his son above him.

He waved frantically.

Brian seemed to rise slightly from his chair. His shadow

leapt gigantically ahead of him, stretching forward and up on the slanting ceiling. Behind his head the glare of the Anglepoise lamp was almost unbearable. Coley was unable to make out the features of his son at all: there was only the silhouette. He couldn't tell if he had noticed anything.

With almost despairing violence he flung the lamp. He saw it speed in a low parabola out over the road which ran parallel to the track, bounce on the white space of Brian's shin exposed above his sock, and vanish in the darkness beyond. The enormous figure rose farther, towering now above the speeding express. Coley was sure now that he had been seen. He made desperate motions with his hands, indicating that he would like a total shut-down of power. The boy waved. Coley turned sick. He stared down at his hands, pathetic little signals of distress. The probability was that the boy couldn't even see them.

But he should have been aware that something was wrong. Surely he must see that.

They tore through another station. They were taking the curves now at speed. They flashed across the scores of intersecting rails of the marshalling yard. The noise was like machine-gun fire. He saw another unit come into play; a two-car diesel slipped away south in a coquettish twinkle of chromium.

'He's showing off,' thought Coley grimly, 'he's going to try to bring every bloody train we've got into motion.'

He knew now that the only way he could save himself would be somehow to get off the train. If only he didn't feel so hellishly bushed.

Coley was never tired. Other people seemed to be tired for him. In every project which he had ever undertaken his adherents had flaked away at some stage, forgotten, like the jettisoned elements in a rocket flight. Hector Coley himself drove on to arrive at his object in perfect condition. But now he was tired, and he felt himself nearing exhaustion with his loss of blood and the battering he had taken.

There was just a chance, he thought, of a stop at Coleyville. The boy had evidently taken in the importance of that one. He'd postpone the final effort to get clear until Coleyville was reached.

He leant over the cold metal of which the log was made, and embraced it like a lover. The metal was cold and refreshing against the skin of face and chest. Through his blurring vision he saw again the great grey plain, and the approaching scissors intersection before Coleyville. Once again the smart little roadster ground to a peremptory halt at the crossing. Other cars halted behind it.

But the express did not this time slacken speed. It went through Coleyville at sixty. For a fleeting instant he saw again the maroon face of the guard, the giant blonde, the malevolence of the middle-aged schoolboy. Those waiting waited still. Those who had been waving waved on. Then Coleyville was gone, and the man on the log recognised that he would have to jump for it. He thought ahead.

Wistfully his mind passed over the swimming pool of the country club. If only that had been water. He winced at the appalling idea of crashing through glass.

But where else could he make it? Spring on to the roof of the tunnel, as they entered? But no, the mountain above was too sheer; it would be like flinging himself against a brick wall. Then he remembered the trees which overhung the long straight beyond. He'd been in the Pullman last time they'd gone under those. But he might be able to grab one and hang from it long enough to let the express pass beneath him.

He fainted away.

When he came to he found that the express was emerging from the tunnel. He wondered how many times he had made the circuit. Several times, probably. Looking across the countryside from this high vantage point he could see on almost every track trains and cars travelling, east, west, south, north.

He felt a cold wind blowing now powerfully across the track. It was horrendous, roaring. It threatened to drag his very hair out by the roots. The shirt sleeves were flapping like mad, trapped seagulls. He twisted his head to face the blast and looked on at the final horror.

His son had quitted the control panel. He was now

squatting, setting a fan on the long grey meadow of carpet. In the whirlwind everything light in the landscape was going over, the waving figures of the yokels and children, the flimsier structures of paper cottages. The station at Coleyville was collapsing, while the people on the platform waited patiently.

Brian smiled. Coley saw him smile.

Then, as he thought that he must be obliged to relinquish his hold and be blown away to destruction, the boy picked the fan up again, and placed it where it always had been.

But he did not return to his seat at the control panel. He went out through the door, and shut it behind him. The noise as it slammed was like a shell exploding.

The express went down the long straight through the suspension bridge and towards the curve at the bottom and reached a hundred miles an hour. Coley watched the overhanging branches of the trees sweep towards him. He climbed on to the logs and steadied himself with his feet braced against a knot to make this last leap. He realised that he would have to make it good the first time, and hoist himself well clear of the onrushing roofs of the following coaches.

Red, yellow, brown, green, the trees suddenly showed.

He made his effort.

He felt the spines run through his hands. Then the branch broke, and he was jammed in the doorway of the next carriage.

He pulled a spine which had remained in his flesh clear, then lay there. He was broken. He waited for the express to derail.

But it did not derail. It swooped on the curve and screamed round it. Almost exuberantly it hurled itself at the next stretch running below the now abandoned control panel. Behind him he heard but did not see the last light trucks and petrol waggons go somersaulting off the track. For a moment there was a grinding check on the express: the wheels raced, then a link must have snapped and the wheels bit again. They surged forward.

The clatter as they started across the marshalling yard

began again.

Coley got up quickly. The will which had devastated board rooms, concentrated now in his tiny figure, was the only part of him which had not been reduced to a scale of one in three hundred. He remembered that before getting on to the express at the outset of this misconceived adventure he had sunk almost to his knees in the foam-rubber ballast on which the track was laid. In the marshalling yard there was acres of it. He stepped back on the log-bearing truck and looked quickly about him.

'Foam-rubber,' he said to himself, 'not ballast.'

He flung himself out, as if into a feather bed.

He lay for a moment luxuriously. He watched the express disappear in the direction of shattered Coleyville. He sighed. What a close thing.

Downstairs, Brian was buckling on his raincoat. His mother watched him anxiously.

'I think your father would prefer it if just this once more you helped him with his trains. It's a bit late to go out.'

'No, he sent me away.'

His mother sighed. She looked forward to an uncomfortable scene with Hector when he should deign to reappear. He probably wouldn't even eat his dinner and then be even more bad-tempered because he was hungry.

'Don't be long, then.'

'I'm only going out to Billy's. We're going to watch for a hedgehog he says comes out at night in his garden.'

'All right then, but be sure to wrap up well.'

Coley hauled himself to his feet. He stood alone, a figure of flesh and blood in a world of fakes.

'I shall never play with them again, not after this,' he said quietly.

It was a decision, but it was accurate also as a prophecy. A sibilant hiss was all he heard of the diesel before it struck him. It was travelling at only three miles an hour, or call it sixty.

It killed him.

Before he died he thought: 'How wretched to die here like this, tiny, probably not even found. They'll wonder whatever became of me.'

He wished he might have been out altogether of the tiny world which had proved to be too big for him. It was his dying wish.

No one doubted that it had been murder when Hector Coley was found stretched out across the toy world which had been his great hobby and pride. But so battered and bloodied and broken a figure could only have resulted from the attack of a maniac of prodigious strength.

'He was still playing with the models when he was surprised,' reported the Inspector. 'The current was on, and about ten of them had come to rest against his body. To be frank, though, he looked as if about ten real ones had hit him.'

THE WOMAN IN THE GREEN DRESS

Joyce Marsh

Life-expectancy statisticians will tell you that you are safer sleeping in a train than you are in your own bed at home. Statistics can be made to prove anything—almost. While the figures may be correct as far as they go, they do not take into account that many people who die in their own bed would be too ill to travel by train, and the figures are 'loaded' in favour of rail travel.

The basic truth is that people who die on trains either die in one of the very infrequent disasters, or as a result of foul-play. In spite of the popular image created by such books and films as Murder on the Orient Express or Double Indemnity, very few murders indeed are committed on trains and those that are are connected with football-hooliganism and similar far-from-romantic activities.

By the very nature of the crime, murder must have Motive, Opportunity and the Means of carrying it out. The latter two are difficult to arrange on a train where the possibility of an unexpected witness or similar circumstance is a constant danger to the murderer.

Traditionally the spirit of the murderer's victim haunts the scene of the crime seeking revenge or atonement. This is all very well when the scene of the crime is a dark, damp gothic castle, but when the scene is a modern, fast-moving railway-car few of the former rules apply. In The Woman in the Green Dress the problem of presenting the apparition and the difficulties of resolving the enigma that has been presented is handled in a deft and novel way.

ALISON TEMPLE STOOD at her kitchen sink washing up. It was always the first chore of her day, and with the ease of long practice she flicked her cloth around the cups and across the saucers and plates. It was not a job that required much concentration and only half her mind was on what she was doing, for the 8.03 from Sutton Street was due at any moment and she was listening for the first sounds of its approach.

Below her and less than fifty yards away the shining bright ribbon of the track snaked away towards Caitham Junction a quarter of a mile or so down the line. Most of her neighbours in the flats complained of the noise, dirt and inconvenience of living so close to the railway line— but not Alison. Even at the age of thirty-six she had never outgrown her childhood pleasure in watching the trains go by.

The huge engines of her childhood days, belching clouds of smoke and steam, had given way to sleek, gleaming diesel locomotives which throbbed with speed as they hurtled over their unending miles of track. There was a tremendous excitement in their monstrous power, but her romantic imagination was, and always had been, most deeply stirred by the passengers briefly glimpsed as they sped on to distant places where she herself had never been. These anonymous travellers fascinated her; without past or future, their lives touched her own for one split second and then were gone, as if they had never existed until that moment and never would again.

She could hear the train now, and by leaning forward and slightly craning her neck she could just see the yellow-nosed diesel coming down the line. It was travelling quite fast, but as usual it began to slow down before reaching her flat and by the time the engine was opposite her window she could see into the carriages quite plainly. The train was not crowded and she gave each carriage a long, concentrated stare. Suddenly out of the corner of her eye she caught a flash of bright green, and she turned her head sharply.

In the second to last carriage a woman wearing a vivid green dress was leaning far out of the window. Her arms waved frantically and her head was strained far back as if someone inside the carriage was pulling at her hair. The train rolled on towards Alison's house, slowly, calmly, and the woman in the green dress struggled desperately against some unseen force.

The carriage came abreast of the window and Alison was looking straight into the woman's eyes. The desperate, urgent fear in those eyes flung across the dividing space until Alison felt it herself in the tightening of the muscles of her throat and the fearful pounding of her heart.

Then with a violent effort the woman in green jerked her head free and throwing herself even further forward she began to struggle with the outside handle of the carriage door. In a brief moment she had succeeded and the door swung open. The horrified watcher at the window saw her gather herself to leap out, but the unseen person in the carriage violently pulled her back, and she was gone from sight. The train passed by the window and only by pressing her face against the glass was Alison able to see the open swinging door—and then, just before it passed out of sight, an arm, a man's arm, reach out to pull it shut.

Alison stood quite still, her face remaining pressed against the cool glass. Every detail of the scene she had just witnessed was sharply etched on her mind. In a few seconds, the first numbing shock had passed, and as the last carriage finally disappeared from view she moved swiftly. She had to warn the station ahead; the train would pull into Caitham Junction in a few minutes and could pull out again before anyone knew of the woman's desperate plight.

The rainbow soap suds still glistened on her hands as Alison fumbled urgently with the telephone directories. The dampness on them made it difficult to turn the pages and with a quick impatient gesture she flung the books on the floor. The police—dial 999—that was the quickest way.

'Which service do you require?'

'The police and please, this is very urgent.'

In less than a minute she was connected to the police. Forcing herself to be very calm, for a wild, incoherent rush of words would only delay the necessary action, Alison gave her name and address first and then, speaking clearly and carefully, briefly explained her call. And that, for the moment, was all she could do for the woman in the green dress.

It was little more than an hour later when the police constable called on her. He was a courteous young man but inclined to be slow and ponderous as he checked the details of her statement. Alison answered carefully, controlling her impatience as best she could until at last she could bear it no longer.

'What about the woman? Were you in time—is she all right?'

The disjointed questions were hurled at him urgently. He looked at her curiously and for what seemed a particularly long time before he answered.

'Madam, there was no trace of a woman answering your description, neither was there any sign of a disturbance in any of the carriages.'

Alison stared at him unbelievingly. Then she said, 'But there must have been, perhaps you searched the wrong train.'

'No, Madam, it was the right train and she was not there. Possibly the lady had left the station by the time we got there.'

'She couldn't have done, she wouldn't have just walked away, not after what I saw happening to her. I tell you that that woman was being violently attacked, I saw it all from the window.'

Alison waved her hand vaguely in the direction of the kitchen window. The policeman made no move to check her viewpoint but he answered politely.

'I am not doubting your word, but perhaps the lady was not in such desperate straits as you imagined. Distance can distort things sometimes, you know.'

There was an air of finality about the way he turned back to his note book which precluded any further discussion. Meekly Alison told her story again, carefully remembering all the details, and after a few more formalities, the policeman left.

For the rest of the day Alison was haunted both by the incident and the woman herself. There had been a curious familiarity about her as if she had seen her somewhere before, perhaps briefly and in some forgotten place. At times Alison closed her eyes and allowed the whole scene to parade before her inner mind whilst she sought to remember every detail of those distorted features.

She wandered restlessly from room to room, unable to concentrate on her work. The flat had suddenly become lonely and desolate and she longed for the moment when her husband would come home.

At first Ted had shown a mild interest, but as soon as he heard of the police theory his interest almost visibly died away.

'Well, that's it then, isn't it? I should forget about it if I were you, it's not your pigeon anyway.'

He turned on the television. His wife knew from past experience that it would be useless to attempt further conversation, and for the rest of the evening she managed to push the incident out of her thoughts.

It was not until the next morning as she was washing up and the sound of the 8.03 first struck her ear, that she thought again of the woman in the green dress. She paused in her work to lean forward as the engine passed the window. Then she saw it—a flash of green and there it was again, the same woman in the same dress leaning from the same carriage window.

In a daze of frightening unreality she watched yesterday's scene re-enacted in precisely the same detail. The

176

vivid green dress shimmered in the misty morning air, the head strained backwards and the arms pawed frantically in a desperate effort to escape the unseen terror inside the carriage. In exactly the same place the door swung open and the woman was pulled back out of sight. Alison watched the unfolding of the drama until the arm reached out to shut the door and then, in a surge of panic, she ran to the telephone.

Gone today were the careful precise sentences with which she had told her story the day before. Now she rambled and shouted into the telephone, desperately compelling her listener to action and somehow she made herself understood. Afterwards she sat very still, trying to think, trying to calm herself. Nothing made any sense. Only one thing was certain—she had seen it, and what she had seen was real and terrifying.

The police did not call this time; they telephoned. It was a conversation which left her trembling with bewilderment, fear and humiliation. Miserably she had heard the cold, curt voice of authority informing her that once again the train had been needlessly delayed and searched, and nothing unusual had been found. There had been a steely edge to the police officer's voice as he had gone on to suggest that the whole incident was probably a foolish hoax.

'It might be as well if you kept away from the window when that train passes. Unless. . . .' His voice trailed off on the word.

'Unless what?' Alison had asked sharply.

'Well . . . never mind. Speak to your husband about it and please, try not to see any more women in green dresses.'

Ted was even less kind. 'For heaven's sake Alison, wrap it up. You heard what the police said, it's just a joke some kids are playing on you and it serves you right, you're always peering into the carriages; people don't like being spied on. Tomorrow you just keep away from the window.'

Ted was not the most patient of men and she could not tell him that the woman was not young, at least not young enough to play practical jokes. The tears smarted in her eyes as she turned to the evening washing up. The tightly drawn curtains were only a flimsy barrier between herself and the suddenly sinister railway.

The next morning she tried very hard not to watch the 8.03 from Sutton Street. She sat rigidly at the kitchen table, afraid of her own window. The first tiny singing rattle heralded the approach of the train. It came closer, the roaring power of the engine throbbed into the room, it was bursting inside her head. The bright green dress seemed to jump and dance before her eyes.

It was unbearable. She flung herself to the window and looked straight down into the tormented eyes of the woman in green. Peering intently. Alison tried to conquer distance so that she could see every detail of the woman's face. There was still something hauntingly familiar about it, but she didn't know what.

Every detail of the macabre charade was played out exactly as it had happened before and exactly as she was to see it again a dozen times or more in the following days.

Alison became accustomed to her fantasy. She no longer tried to avoid the window when the 8.03 went by. Morning after morning, with a curious detached interest, she watched the tormented struggles of the woman in green, paying such close attention that almost daily she saw tiny new details which she had not noticed before.

But she never spoke to anyone of the woman in the green dress again; not to Ted and certainly not to the police. Instead she thought about her for hours at a time and one strange, confused thought ran through her mind over and over again. For one brief moment every morning her life became inextricably entwined with the strange woman on the train; but if that moment was not now ... when was it?

Then the idea came to her quite suddenly. She would take a bus to Sutton Street and board the 8.03 and if the woman existed then Alison would find her on the train.

It had not been easy to find an excuse for leaving the flat so early and Ted had looked surprised. But she had managed it, and now she was at Sutton Street, waiting with mounting excitement for the train. She hastily looked over the other passengers on the platform; the woman was certainly not amongst them. The train rolled slowly into the station; a few people ran through the barrier at the last moment, but these were all men.

Alison was unable to resist her urge to start at the very front of the train and look in at every carriage window. Her heart beat faster as she approached the second to last carriage; with a slight shock of disappointment she saw that it contained only one passenger—a man. The very last carriage was occupied by noisy Cubs and Scouts off on an outing.

The whistle blew as the train was about to pull out. There was no time for hesitation. Impulsively she opened the door of the second to last carriage and jumped in.

The man, not old but not young either, sat hunched in his corner. He neither stirred nor looked up as Alison sat down opposite him. Suddenly she wished that she had not chosen this carriage. There was something frighteningly disconcerting in his total disregard of her and in his utter stillness. She even leant a little towards him to stare into his face, and still he did not move. She tore her eyes away from him and the next moment flung a hand over her mouth to stifle a little involuntary scream.

There had been no sound of the door opening and the train was already moving quite fast, yet now, suddenly and inexplicably, there was someone else in the carriage. On the opposite seat, in the far corner was a woman—a woman in a bright green dress, its glowing, exotic colour seeming iridescent against the dingy red seats. The woman was wearing a hat now, a black hat with a large soft brim curving gracefully down over her face. Everything she wore seemed bright and new, from the black hat, the shiny black shoes and the vivid dress to the black leather handbag on her arm. At least, everything was new except her gloves. They were old and so worn that several of the finger tips showed pinkly through the holes.

The woman seemed very conscious of these gloves for she was staring down at them with fixed attention, her body as rigid and unmoving as the man in the corner seat.

The bright dress seemed curiously static; it was not even rising and falling as she breathed. Then Alison realised that they were not breathing: the man and the woman both sat absolutely still, like photographs projected onto the thick dusty backcloth of the carriage.

Since her first startled gesture Alison herself had not moved and she now felt as if she had been rendered as motionless as her two companions. She tried to speak but it was an immense effort and the words oozed slowly from her lips.

'Who ... are ... you?'

Neither of them gave any sign that they had seen or heard her. She turned her head. Through the window Alison saw the wood yard which was only a mile or so from her home. In a few minutes they would be passing the flat. It was then that they moved, both together and at first with curious little jerks like puppets. The man straightened himself and the woman began plucking at her gloves, trying to fold over the fabric to hide the holes.

The man edged along the seat; he was leaning sideways onto an outstretched arm which was now only inches away from the woman's handbag. He began fumbling with the catch, but it was new and stiff. The bag jerked on her arm and the woman, now aware of what he was doing, snatched it away. The man's face changed expression, and became vicious. Abandoning pretence, he grabbed the bag with one hand and with the other hit her such a blow that her head jerked back and the black hat fell off to be trampled underfoot as they struggled for the bag; and still Alison could not see the woman's face, nor force her own heavy body to move except with exasperating slowness.

The green dress danced past her as the woman let go the bag and flung herself towards the window. She leaned far out and her arms waved frantically in the air.

The man was alarmed. He dropped the bag and leapt towards her, grabbing her hair violently so that her head jerked back. Something shone coldly bright in his hand as he punched her back, once, twice, three times. A dark red stain appeared and grew larger on the back of the dress.

Alison tried to stand up, but although her body obeyed her will, it did so slowly, so very slowly. She wanted to interfere but she knew that she could not.

The woman had the door open and although her blood was spilling down on to the floor, she was gathering her last strength to leap out. They were opposite the flat and Alison looked out over the woman's head to see her own kitchen window with all its sweet familiarity, the old faded curtains and even the jam jar soaking on the sill. But someone was standing at her sink. At first the figure was blurred and indistinct, then it leaned forward and Alison saw her own face pressed against the glass.

The sight brought her an overwhelming surge of relief. This nightmare in the carriage was nothing to do with her. It was their present and not hers. In her own present moment she was where she should be—washing up at her kitchen sink. She sighed and closed her eyes, exhausted.

When she opened them again another face was peering down into hers, a face framed by a stiff white cap.

'Are you feeling better, dear?'

'I don't know,' Alison answered. 'Where am I?'

'You were found unconscious in one of the carriages. You're in the waiting room at Caitham Junction.'

They took her home in a car, but she would not let them send for Ted or a doctor. She wanted to be alone, alone to think. What had she been doing on the train? Where had she been going and why?

She thought about it for a long time. She remembered going to bed the night before but then ... nothing. She couldn't even remember why she had got on the train.

Perhaps Ted would know. No; she knew that she must not say anything at all about it to her husband.

The dirty breakfast dishes were still stacked in the sink and automatically she began to wash up. A fast express train roared into view and Alison dropped the cup she was holding, pressed her hands over her ears and screamed. Her screams grew louder, matching the roaring crescendo of the train....

The days grew into weeks and then months. The soft

warm spring turned to a blazing summer which burned itself out into autumn. Alison no longer watched the trains go by. A heavy Venetian blind hung at the window and its slats were always turned down, making it so dark in the kitchen that she had to use electric light even in the middle of the day. Sometimes, especially in the early morning, the sound of a train made her sweat and tremble with an incomprehensible terror. Although occasionally she forgot her fear of the trains it was never for long. She would sit for hours brooding, groping in her mind for a memory, a memory that she did not want to recall but knew she must if she were ever to dispel the hazy frightening confusion into which she had sunk.

Although she did not realise it, Alison had grown thin and gaunt. Her pinched white face with its hollow cheeks and dark-rimmed eyes were almost unrecognisable. Ted often looked at her with anxious, puzzled sympathy, for she told him nothing and he had no idea why his wife seemed so disturbed and ill, but a plan had begun to form in his mind.

He was a simple man and he thought he had found a simple solution to Alison's unspoken troubles. He came home one evening with his arms full of packages and his face glowing with the excitement of a schoolboy.

'Come here, little lady. Have I got a surprise for you.'

She came at once, smiling at his enthusiasm.

'We are going on a holiday,' he announced, 'a proper holiday. Everything's booked and we're off tomorrow for a whole week in Majorca.'

He paused dramatically: neither of them had ever been abroad before and Alison caught some of his excitement.

'I've been planning this for weeks and I thought of everything,' he said. 'I have even bought you a complete new outfit to go away in—just like another honeymoon.'

He began to open his parcels and laid out his purchases one by one on the kitchen table. A pair of shiny black shoes, an expensive, real leather handbag, a black hat with a large soft brim and, last of all, a bright green dress.

Alison recoiled; the vague memory exploded into a terrifying flash of clarity.

'Oh, damn, I forgot the gloves,' Ted was saying. 'Still, I expect you've got an old pair of black gloves somewhere.'

She stared at him desperately, but he did not notice and as she looked into his plain simple face she knew he would not understand. He was happily explaining away some small difficulty.

'So you see, love, I'll have to meet you later at the airport terminal. Take a taxi to Sutton Street and catch the 8.03.'

Alison stood very still on the station platform. The silky material of the green dress caressed her skin and the black hat framed and softened her face, making her look quite young and pretty again.

Last night she had decided not to wear the dress or to be on this train. Even this morning her conscious mind had urged her to burn the dress and lock herself in the bedroom. But even as she thought of it Alison had known that she would wear the dress and that she would be on the 8.03 from Sutton Street. Whatever was to happen to her in this dress had already happened sometime in her future and she could not change it any more than she could go back and change her past. Every last detail had been right, even to her old black gloves with the holes in the fingers, which contrasted sharply with the smart newness of her other clothes.

The train came into the platform. The last carriage stopped in front of her but it was full of Cubs and Scouts on an outing, just as she had known it would be.

There was one man in the next carriage and he did not look up as she got in. Alison looked down at her hands, and the old worn gloves irritated her.

The train moved off and she became very occupied with her gloves as she tried to fold over the fabric to hide the holes. They were passing the wood-yard and she knew the man would begin to edge his hand close to her bag.

With daunting certainty she knew his every move. She felt the stinging blow to her head and then they were struggling and fighting in the swaying carriage.

'I am not here, this is not me,' she heard herself

shouting the words aloud. The train was passing the flats, soon she would be able to see her kitchen window.

'I know I shall be there, standing at my window, washing up.' She screamed the words and tore herself free from his grasping hands to fling herself at the window.

The heavy blow struck her back once and then again and again, and she felt the hot sticky blood trickle down her legs. Excruciating pains tore her body and through red swirling mists she looked up at her window with a desperate hope.

The Venetian blind was drawn up and there was no one there. The window gazed back at her, starkly empty. Hopelessly she leaned far out and the door of the train swung open. She felt him jerk her back and as oblivion rushed in upon her, past present and future gathered together to make one final moment of life for the woman in the green dress.

THE VERY SILENT TRAVELLER

Paul Tabori

After expanding into Europe the British railway builders turned their attention to the American continent. The USA had its own engineers (which is a subject for another book), but British engineers built Canada's Grand Trunk Railway, which was almost a financial disaster. South America saw the combining of the talents of both British and US engineers, notably Thomas Brassey and William Wheelwright, a US shipper and promoter of copper and coal mining. Together they built almost two hundred miles of railway from Rosario to Cordoba that was called the Central Argentine Railway. Wheelwright knew the language and the people, so most of the executive work of the enterprise fell to him. Starting in 1863 and lasting seven years, the route lay mostly over bare, stony ground so that it was possible to lay the sleepers directly upon it, with a draining ditch at each side of the line.

It was not a well-run railway. It had been built with British money and had a British board of directors who ineffectively tried to control it from London. This fact, and the ever-changing balance of power in South America caused by war and revolution, made train travel a hazardous business.

Paul Tabori fully understood the situation when he wrote the following very short, very gristly, but highly amusing story of **The Very Silent Traveller.**

THE SQUAT FUNNEL of the engine gave a choking, gurgling sound. It spat myriads of fiery sparks into the pitch-coloured night. The comet's tail of the sparks was like a woman's mane, spreading along the length of the clattering train—a wavering, fading and recurrent magic carpet, broken and reunited as the rush of the coaches created an irregular slipstream, now narrowing at the curves, now spreading out again on the straight stretches. Behind the train the sparks settled on the black soil, blinked briefly and then died one by one as they touched the cool earth.

A row of lights appeared in the night. The train began to slow down, brakes bit on wheels, the roaring and panting became less strident. The three-toned whistle gave a long shriek as the glimmer of the second set of signals streaked by.

The engine pulled up, pulsating and burbling steam, at a small station on the edge of the vast Argentine plains. The station was marked by half-a-dozen apple-trees: the name of it, on a faded and battered piece of corrugated iron, was scarcely visible. The sheet of iron had been fastened with wire between two of the trees to secure it against the violent winter storms. There was no platform, no hut, no telegraphist's shack. Apart from the sign wired to the trees and a few forlorn oil-lamps there was nothing to signify a stop. The nearest station on the line with a permanent staff was at least thirty miles away.

The halt was brief; little more than three minutes. The engine spewed forth another column of fiery sparks, emitting a cloud of steam. Then the wheels began to turn again; the choking, gurgling, panting sounds were repeated and the shrill whistle pierced the night.

In this brief interval one passenger boarded the train. Or rather, he was helped up the steep iron steps by three others who were evidently seeing him off. They supported him along the corridor and placed him in an empty compartment. Then, without any good-byes or last-minute talk, they jumped from the train. The wheels were already moving and they barely had time to regain the ground before the train pulled out. It would seem a case of bad manners—yet the three men had a good excuse for not lingering.

Transporting dead bodies in the Argentine used to be an extremely costly and difficult business. Red tape indeed made it almost impossible; it needed six different kinds of permits, a dozen declarations, a pile of documents. All this became even more difficult in districts where the simple ranches, the scattered *estancias*, were fifty or a hundred miles from the nearest town. Not even the fastest horse could carry the messengers to collect the necessary permits within the two or three days during which a corpse could be preserved. And if, by some lucky chance, the permits were forthcoming, the railway company charged ten times as much for a dead traveller as for a living one—not to mention the expense of the coffin and the ticket of the attendant, who under the company rules, had to accompany such a consignment. Many of the ranchers lived well without having more than a small fund of cash; more than one would have been ruined by such a heavy expenditure. Yet they were loath to bury their relatives on their own farms, especially if there was a family mausoleum in Buenos Aires.

But luckily there was still some ingenuity and enterprise left in these parts, and the traveller who boarded the train at the wayside halt was making his trip because of such ingenuity. He was very dead indeed; but his pious and grief-stricken relatives simply smuggled him onto the express. They wrapped him up well and pushed his sombrero over his forehead; by supporting him closely, they made any possible observer believe that he was an invalid or maybe a little drunk. One of them then settled the price of the ticket with the conductor, tipping him well so that the 'poor invalid' should be left undisturbed and in sole possession of the compartment.

As soon as the train had pulled out, another of the three men jumped on a horse and rode off post-haste to the nearest telegraph office, twenty miles away. There he sent a telegram to the dead man's uncle in Buenos Aires, giving him the number of the coach and compartment in which the corpse was travelling. Uncle Felipe was to meet the train at the terminus and take care of the rest.

The other two men remained standing near the track, staring after the rapidly-disappearing red tail lights. They felt very solemn—but also considerably relieved.

At the next stop—a much bigger one—Captain Grodeck boarded the train.

The Captain had started life in the Imperial German Army but owing to some slight misunderstanding over cards (a fifth ace had unaccountably got into the pack) he was obliged to resign his commission. He had had some hard times after that, but later found his perfect niche in promoting revolutions. They needed little promoting in South and Central America—except that the captain was organising them strictly for the benefit of his employers, a large and prosperous armaments group.

Just now he was on his way back from Paraguay, after a very profitable stay. He had a lot of baggage which he had to lug down the corridor himself. By the time he had finished the chore he was bathed in sweat, his scarred face glistening with it; and he was in a vile temper. Cursing, panting and shouting, he expressed most unflattering opinions about the Argentinian railway system in general and the lack of porters in particular. He dwelt with venomous intensity on the high steps of the carriages and the time-table of the only southbound express train that made a night journey inevitable.

He continued his loud outburst outside each crowded compartment. He was forced to drag his suitcase, boxes and rugs along the swaying narrow corridors—there was nowhere an empty seat.

Finally he reached the compartment in which the silent traveller was ensconced in solitary splendour. He was sitting in the darkest corner, huddled up, limp. The broadbrimmed black sombrero had slipped down to the tip of his nose. The blue-shaded reading lamp threw a pale circle of light upon him. He seemed to be sleeping soundly, lost in a happier world of dreams.

'Do you mind señor?' asked Captain Grodeck.

There was no answer. He pushed his way into the compartment, distributing his luggage with considerable noise; then switched on the central light and, sitting down, inspected his fellow-traveller.

The huddled passenger sat modestly and quietly in his corner. There was little to be seen of his face—except that he had not shaved for some time. His cloak reached to the ground, enveloping his body; both hands were buried in the large patch pockets. The rhythmic shaking of the train made the body tremble and sway gently.

Captain Grodeck took the seat opposite. As he had become quite wrought-up with his passionate denunciations, he knew he couldn't sleep. So he decided to have some intelligent conversation—or just conversation.

Politely he asked a number of questions in his execrable Spanish. When he received no reply, he tried other languages—Portuguese, French, English, even his native German. But this linguistic effort proved all unavailing. His travelling companion sat there, stubbornly silent, clumsily immobile.

Captain Grodeck was a persistent man. He produced his pig-skin cigar-case, selected the finest, speckled Havana and held it out invitingly. He praised its quality, its aroma; he hoped that the señor would accept it as a token of friendship.

There was no answer.

The captain made two other attempts to make the silent traveller speak. But it was all in vain. Neither polite remarks, nor friendly questions nor offers of cigar and cigarette brought any response.

And now Captain Grodeck discovered that though he had a mass of luggage and was equipped with every convenience for a long journey, he had failed to provide himself with the simplest necessity. He had no matches: his lighter was empty. A cigar between his thick lips, he felt himself all over, reaching into every pocket—but he did not find a single match.

He turned to his companion. 'Could I trouble you for a light?' he asked. But there was no reply.

This final discourtesy made Captain Grodeck see red. He jumped up, bent over the silent stranger and started to shake him with all his might. The lifeless head was knocked several times against the back of the seat, the captain shouting and cursing at him.

Under the powerful grip of the German's hands, the huddled man slid sideways. His sombrero slipped back until it was barely clinging to the back of his head. His hands emerged from the deep pockets; then his whole body suddenly jerked forward, and like a bag of sand it dropped heavily on to the floor of the compartment. The hat rolled away and Grodeck needed no second glance to tell him that the traveller was dead.

Startled and horrified, he stared at the body. He knew his own hot ungovernable temper and had cursed it a thousand times whenever it got him into a scrape. But he had not expected *this*. After all, he had just given the man a good shaking and knocked his silly head a few times against the wall. . . .

But his hesitation only lasted a few moments. With a sudden decision, he bent down and lifted the corpse from the floor. He dragged it to the window and propped it up while he opened the sliding glass. Then, with a mighty heave, he let it drop into the pitch-dark night.

The train rattled on, unconcerned, its wheels devouring the miles.

Early in the morning the express arrived in Buenos Aires.

Uncle Felipe had been waiting for the last hour. Excited and anxious, he elbowed his way through the large crowd until he found the carriage which had been indicated in the telegram.

His plan was all ready. He would board the train, enter

the compartment, 'discover' the dead man and shout for help. . . . But, of course, it would be too late; his poor, dear nephew had died somewhere on the way.

But he searched in vain: there was no trace of his relative in the compartment nor in the whole carriage. Thinking that he had made a mistake, he explored the other carriages. They were all empty now—except for one man with a scarred face and a military bearing who was still lugging some of his heavy suitcases down to the platform. He was just collecting the last piece—from the very compartment in which Uncle Felipe's nephew was supposed to have travelled.

'Excuse me, sir,' Uncle Felipe addressed him. 'Did you have a fellow-passenger in this compartment?'

'Oh yes,' replied Captain Grodeck with a completely expressionless face.

'And?' Uncle Felipe waited breathlessly.

'Oh, he got off about three stations back,' the captain answered and, picking up his last suitcase, descended from the carriage. He made his way along the platform, unconcerned and self-assured while Uncle Felipe crossed himself three times and collapsed in a dead faint.

TAKE THE Z TRAIN

A. V. Harding

The North American contemporary of Charles Dickens was of course Edgar Allen Poe; editor, poet and master of the macabre short story. Poe was editor of the Southern Literary Messenger in 1835, the Burton's Gentleman's Magazine in 1839 and the weekly paper Broadway Journal in 1845. Both men met together in Philadelphia in 1842 when Poe was at his literary peak. When he died at the early age of forty neither of them had conceived the idea of a macabre railway story.

It was not until 1923 that the macabre story came into its own in North America when Clark Henneberger, a Chicago publisher, produced a pulp magazine entitled Weird Tales with the avowed intention of printing stories in the Poe tradition. Editorship was first offered to H. P. Lovecraft who declined the office; but it was taken up by Farnsworth Wright who, nursing this unique magazine through many troubles, delighted his readers until 1940.

The magazine closed down in September 1954 after thirty-two years in publication during which time hundreds of macabre short stories saw print and at least a dozen authors became established in the field. Yet, I have only been able to select one story that is suitable for the theme of this book.

The first subway in North America was a two-mile length of cut-and-cover tunnel in Boston, built between 1895 and 1898 and intended for street-cars only. New York City had built an experimental tunnel in the lower Broadway area, only 312 feet long, in 1870, which was a failure and was destroyed. The first real subway ran from City Hall to Broadway and 145th Street and opened as late as 1904. Take the Z Train did not appear until the March 1950 issue of Weird Tales but it reflects the atmosphere of the subway forty years earlier.

THE SEER HAD said—all things of certain wisdom and uncertain origin would derive so well from seers—'At the end, the old look back to relive and see again the pattern of their lives. But the young, peculiarly favoured by a destiny which otherwise seems to have neglected them, look searchingly forward, and for this brief instant of eternity see truly what would have been ahead—before the light snuffs out.'

It was a few minutes past five when Henry Abernathy left the office. It was always a few minutes past five when Henry Abernathy left the office. By that time he had taken care of the overflow of work which somehow always found its way to his desk toward the end of the working day and had put away his seersucker coat in the General Employees' Locker.

Longer ago than it would do to remember, Henry had been pleased by the title of Junior Assistant Supervisor of Transportation. He was Assistant all right—to everybody in the office—Supervisor of nothing, and Junior—that was a laugh, with the gray in his hair and the stooped shoulders!

As usual, Henry walked three blocks directly south from the office to the subway station, stopping only for the evening paper at the corner stand. It was all quite as usual. But he had been telling himself all day that this was an important day. He was going to break clean from the old life.

From the earliest, a phrase had been running through his head. It ran in well-worn channels for he had thought this thought before, he knew, though its authorship was obscure. The seer had said ... and the quotation, for that it must be, fascinated him, he knew not why, he'd never known why. Henry Abernathy had believed before in the clean break from his meaningless routine, from the same old faces at the office, the same stupid tasks, the same fear that lashed him with its thongs of insecurity to his humble position.

Thinking this way took him down the metal-tipped subway stairs, through the turnstile and onto the lower level where he waited for his train as he had, it seemed, thousands of times before.

He was suddenly struck with this dim, twinkle-lit cavern way, beneath the perimeter of the earth's surface. The people around him, the steel girders holding the rest of the world from tumbling in upon him, the gum machines, the penny scales ... all these seemed to go out of focus with his concentration on his inner thinkings.

Through instinct he watched the black hole to his left at the end of the platform. He watched more closely, narrowly, as first the noise and then the flickering something away in the tunnel came closer, still closer. He looked up, he knew not why for it was a completely irrelevant act, at the ceiling of the underground station. It seemed, in the subterranean gloom, as far away as the top of the universe.

He was tired, he supposed. Supposed? He *knew*. Life does that to you, doesn't it? To everyone. Abernathy wondered if those around him were as miserable as he was, or if their misery was an unrecognised, locked-up something deep inside. For this underground tomb was a place for reflection, although conversely, in its bustle and noisome urgency, humans could take a holiday from their consciences, and pushing, wriggling, hurrying off and on these mechanised moles that bore them to and from their tasks, forget, and in the forgetting be complacent.

Times before beyond counting when Henry Abernathy had waited here like this for his A or B train, he'd thought that people must age faster in such an alien environment—the so-hard, yieldless platform, the dank air, the

196

farness away from things that counted like sky and sun and wind. He wondered if people like himself didn't surely age more rapidly in a subway tomb like this where neither hope nor anything else could grow or flourish.

The dull metal thing slid into the station, its caterpillar length bucking with shrill, rasping protests, its garish-lit cars beckoning. The doors slid open and Henry Abernathy walked automatically forward, glancing as he always did—for he was a meticulous man—at the square in the window that gave the alphabetical letter of the train. There were only two that came to this platform—the A, which was an express and the B, a local. Both would get him home.

He was aboard with the doors slid silently closed behind him and the train jerking, jumping to life again; he was sitting on the uncomfortable cane seats when what he had just automatically glanced at in the identification square on the outside window took form in his mind. So strongly that he got up and walked over to the window and looked at the letter in reverse. It glowed smally against the moving black background of tunnel, for they were out of the station now. It said plainly, so there could be no mistake, Z train.

The subway shook with its gathering speed, and Henry went back to his seat. It was most peculiar. Never before had any but an A or B train run on this track. He'd never heard of a Z train! Why . . . he didn't even know where he was going!

He sat with his hands clasped in his lap and felt, on the other side of the wonder, a relief that may be this was the beginning of his adventure. The train lurched and zoomed on, and as the moments ticked away ominously, he realised that the underground monster fled headless and heedless without the reprieve of those occasional light oases in the dreadful night of the subway. Surely they would have come to another station by now! Then . . . wait a moment more. Certainly by *now*! This, then, was his adventure! This was the difference that would, despite himself and his own weakness to effect the change, *any* change, alter the course for him. That part he gloated over—no more boss, no more regular hours. . . .

The train was going faster. It has been a monotonous life, Henry Abernathy, he told himself. Monotonous and quite terrible. He could confess to himself now something that he would never do in the sunshine or on the street that was somewhere miles above him and this rushing thing that bore him on. He would confess that he had thought of self-destruction.

A clamminess came over him. The air from the tunnel was dank as it whistled in an open window at the other end of the car. It was a very long way between stations, and at this speed, that wasn't right!

He sought out other faces for reassurance. Somehow, quite suddenly, there seemed to be so few of them, and with those, the eyes were averted or hidden behind bundles or papers. Abernathy cleared his throat to test his voice. He would say to someone—the nearest person— 'Beg pardon, but what train am I on?' Now wasn't that a silly question! He was sitting nearly directly across from the window whereon the identification plate was set, and the plate said so clearly—Z train.

He sat more stiffly against the seat back, tension taking hold of him and ramrodding his body. It was his imagination that said that the train plunged forward eagerly into the ever-greater darkness of the unfolding tunnel, for a train doesn't plunge eagerly—not even a Z train! A poetic liberty, a figment of the imagination!

Henry fixed his eyes on the nearest person to him—a very young man with books and sweater, obviously just from school, an eager young man, so eager. With dreams, Henry Abernathy thought with a kind of sadness. The young man was looking at nothing particularly, and Abernathy thought, Ah, soon he will look at me. I shall catch his eye and say, leaning forward so I don't have to advertise it to the whole rest of the car, 'Young man, I seem to have gotten on the wrong train'—a small smile at my own stupidity—'but just *where* are we going?'

But the young man in the sweater would not look his

way. He tapped his books with his fingertips, tapped his foot on the floor, whistled through his teeth and looked out the window or up and down the car, casually, swiftly.

Abernathy got up to speak to him directly then thought better of it. He passed by close enough to see that the youngster was cleaner than most. He rather imagined *he* had looked something like that on his way home from school years ago, but that was far from here in both time and space.

There was a girl, a pretty girl, he noticed—for he was not too old to miss those things—wide-set eyes, a good chin, nice mouth, well-dressed. He would ask her, but of course one didn't do that. With other men in the car, it would look ... well, *forward* if he directed his inquiries to a pretty young girl.

There were several other men, heavy set, semi-successful or better, watch chains over their paunches, brief-cases—the business type. Bosses. They reminded him so. . . .

Then nearly at the door that opened between the cars there was another man, youngish, in an ill-fitting tuxedo, probably going to a party. It was a rented tuxedo, Henry Abernathy thought to himself with some satisfaction. He knew what *that* was, all right! Why, when he'd been just about that age, he'd once rented a tuxedo and it probably had looked no better on him than it did on this fellow.

Abernathy reached the door and clutched at the reddish-yellow brass knob. It had the reassuring feel of all of life, of reality with the stickiness from scores of hands; people opening and closing it, walking forward, walking back, touching it with their hands.

He went forward then, adding his steps to the speed of the train in that direction. Was it one, two, or three cars, he wasn't sure, nor was he of the other passengers. He staggered a little to the rocking of the subway beneath him. He yearned suddenly to be rid of this thing—this scene, this place. All those figures, those persons he'd sat with in the first car took on a strange, nightmarish familiarity in his mind.

It was the drudgery, the overwork, and the hopelessness of his life that made him this way, he excused, like other people say, 'Something I ate.'

That was what made him *know* that the young boy with the sweater was Henry Abernathy, and so too perhaps, was the slightly older man in the rented tuxedo. The girl was the *she* who had said no. That was long ago too. And those men, those out-of-shape pudgy, expensive cigar-smoking men, were the bosses he'd worked for and others he hadn't worked for, who had given him a glance and dismissal with a look as being beneath them and unworthy of their attention.

The fullness of horror overtook Henry Abernathy as he reached the front of the first car. He leaned against the motorman's compartment and looked ahead at the tunnel rushing onto them and around them. The tunnel curved away, curved away, always turning, it seemed, as though they were going in a circle.

Henry stood and watched fascinated. He could go no further. He could not go back. He looked curiously into the motorman's cubicle. That place was dark, the shade drawn nearly to the bottom of the window.

But there was a man in there with a motorman's cap, and a gloved hand rested on the throttle pulled full open . . . a man who swayed with the motion of the train he drove. A motorman.

The years came back to Henry like leaves falling in sequence, and those people back there behind him were all parts of it, of himself and of others he had known. This train then was what? His life from beginning to end and his destiny?

He stood hypnotised by his thoughts, drawn by the dark fascination of the tunnel ahead, the little yellow lights that flashed by, marking with their feebleness both space and speed. It was an eternity that Henry Abernathy stood there . . . or it was one second. It mattered neither.

But ahead, finally, he saw something. It was not exactly a station, but there was a light, a small flickering light set in the side of the tunnel, and they seemed now instead of rushing towards it, to float towards it.

The screeching, groaning, complaining shrieks of the subway at high speed died away so that they must be slowing down. The light came nearer. There was a sign, a very big sign. He'd seen them before on the occasion when a crowded train at rush hour stops between stations in the darkness of the tunnel and the sign, perhaps pointing or indicating a nearby stairway that leads to the above—the sign says 'Exit'.

There was a sign here under the light. But look, there was more. Across the tracks there was something. He watched intently during the hours it seemed that it took their train to roll closer. It mattered not which he saw first, in what order he perceived these things—the sign, the thing on the tracks; the thing on the tracks, the sign.

It was a body on the tracks, lying face upward fully across them like a sack of something. The face was strangely luminous in the tunnel's darkness, and that face was as terribly familiar as those others behind him in the train. And it was so *right* and so *of course* that the sign under the flickering, yellow light simply read 'Z'.

They were close now, within a couple of rapid pulse beats; the body nearly under the metal monster; the sign, the Z of it growing larger and larger.

And then there was a blinding flash—all the brightness of all the world, of all time exploding in the tunnel, across the so-familiar face and body and Z sign, into the train, into him and his head, touching chords and notes that came out like music—that's what it was—music, easy to hear as it played around and around.

It was the sound of the carousel, the Calliope, and as the little series of whistles, played by keys like an organ, popped and hooted, Henry Abernathy went around and around in the sea of remembering on the gaily painted horse—a horse that fed and brightened itself on his tears of joy and pleasure.

This was an important train day for Henry. He was going to break clean from the old life, and perhaps the old life started—or the only part of it that counted started—on the floor at home with the cream-coloured walls that

201

seemed so tall at the age of seven.

And though he was much beyond it, there were blocks on the floor. He was to spell something out with them, and Mother was persistent. It was a word, a meaningless word, that matters not among the thousands in our language. He was perverse, and there was one letter he would not add, but Mother was so persistent.

'Think!' she said. 'Think!'

And he remembered the deepening colour of her face, remembered it as he remembered now all these other things, past and future.

'Think!' she repeated. 'Think!'

One letter he had to add to make the word perfect, to fill it out for her adult mind to correctness.

'Think!' she said again. *'It's an unusual letter!'*

He knew the letter so well. He had but to push it into place with his foot or his hand. But revolt stayed him.

And then Mother said darkly: 'Think, Henry! Do it or you don't go to the fair!'

And with that the roulette wheel completed its final spin and stopped, marking its choice, and he, petulantly and still unwilling but broken down by the knowledge that he would lose something greater, kicked the letter into place.

And she smiled with the victory and said, 'Of course! Z! You knew it all the time, Henry!'

It was later, then, that he had gone to the carnival almost exploding with his small-child excitement. Was there enough time for all the things that had to be done and seen, touched and played with? Was there enough of him to smell and eat all the things to be smelled and eaten?

And at the end, the best of all—the merry-go-round, on the horses that went *up* and down, *up* and down, round and round, with the strange, strange wonderful music of the Calliope—he would travel miles on his green and yellow horse even as Mother stood outside the world of his race-track and gestured and seemed to stamp her foot, wanting him to stop and making motioning noises.

It was then—sometime during his umpteenth ride on

the bucking green and yellow merry-go-round horse—
then so that his seven-year-old mind knew well the
whispering sounds of the Calliope organ, then that
something had come out of another world, it seemed—a
thing of crashing noise and blinding light; a thing prefaced
only by a little wetness and Mother's anger as she stood,
no longer controlling him, already completely outside of
his world, under a hastily raised umbrella, stamping her
foot and calling to him.

Henry was caught up then in that instant by his friend,
who took him in this time of greatest joy bursting like the
nod of a flower. It was for that moment that the seer had
spoken ... that the Calliope played ... that Z was
remembered.

It was that moment that showed him how it would have
been in times yet unborn, to be forgotten forever in time
never to be. . . .

THE THIRD LEVEL

Jack Finney

The process of building railways in North America began very much as it had in England, the two main governing factors being the constructon of short local lines by private companies and the competition with the systems of canal transport. At first the locomotives were imported from England, but it soon became clear that locomotives designed for a country where coal and anthracite was plentiful for fuel were not going to be practical on a continental basis where wood-fuel was plentiful.

Nevertheless, the network quickly grew. In the South, the South Carolina Railroad opened in 1833 with 136 miles of track from Charleston to Hanburg. In the North, the Western Railroad of Massachusetts ran from Boston to the Erie Canal in 1842. Then the Civil War reduced development so that the 30,500 miles of track built by 1860 had only been increased by a further 3,500 miles by 1864.

Amalgamation of the railroads then began and the canals became obsolescent. The most striking example of this was the combination of the New York Central and Hudson River Railroads during the 1860s by Cornelius Vanderbilt. He built new track on the roads beside the canals and river to make a through-line from New York to the lake.

This was the beginning of the golden age—and not only of the railroads for some. Jack Finney is noted for stories of high imagination. In The Third Level you will find that Grand Central Station is the starting point for a journey you never expected—and might well wish to take.

THE PRESIDENTS OF the New York Central and the New York, New Haven and Hartford railroads will swear on a stack of timetables that there are only two. But I say there are three, because I've *been* on the third level at Grand Central Station. Yes, I've taken the obvious step: I talked to a psychiatrist friend of mine, among others. I told him about the third level at Grand Central Station, and he said it was a waking-dream wish fulfilment. He said I was unhappy. That made my wife kind of mad, but he explained that he meant the modern world is full of insecurity, fear, war, worry, and all the rest of it, and that I just wanted to escape. Well, hell, who doesn't? Everybody I know wants to escape, but they don't wander down into any third level at Grand Central Station.

But that's the reason, he said, and my friends all agreed. Everything points to it, they claimed. My stamp collecting, for example—that's a 'temporary refuge from reality'. Well, maybe, but my grandfather didn't need any refuge from reality; things were pretty nice and peaceful in his day, from all I hear, and he started my collection. It's a nice collection, too, blocks of four of practically every US issue, first-day covers, and so on. President Roosevelt collected stamps, too, you know.

Anyway, here's what happened at Grand Central. One night last summer I worked late at the office. I was in a hurry to get uptown to my apartment, so I decided to subway from Grand Central because it's faster than the bus.

Now, I don't know why this should have happened to me. I'm just an ordinary guy named Charley, thirty-one years old, and I was wearing a tan gabardine suit and a straw hat with a fancy band—I passed a dozen men who looked just like me. And I wasn't trying to escape from anything; I just wanted to get home to Louisa, my wife.

I turned into Grand Central from Vanderbilt Avenue and went down the steps to the first level, where you take trains like the Twentieth Century. Then I walked down another flight to the second level, where the suburban trains leave from, ducked into an arched doorway heading for the subway—and got lost. That's easy to do. I've been in and out of Grand Central hundreds of times, but I'm always bumping into new doorways and stairs and corridors. Once I got into a tunnel about a mile long and came out in the lobby of the Roosevelt Hotel. Another time I came up in an office building on the Forty-sixth Street, three blocks away.

Sometimes I think Grand Central is growing like a tree, pushing out new corridors and staircases like roots. There's probably a long tunnel that nobody knows about feeling its way under the city right now, on its way to Times Square, and maybe another to Central Park. And maybe—because for so many people through the years Grand Central *has* been an exit, a way of escape—maybe that's how the tunnel I got into ... but I never told my psychiatrist friend about that idea.

The corridor I was in began angling left and slanting downward and I thought that was wrong, but I kept on walking. All I could hear was the empty sound of my own footsteps and I didn't pass a soul. Then I heard that sort of hollow roar ahead that means open space, and people talking. The tunnel turned sharp left; I went down a short flight of stairs and came out on the third level at Grand Central Station. For just a moment I thought I was back on the second level, but I saw the room was smaller, there were fewer ticket windows and train gates, and the information booth in the centre was wood and old-looking. And the man in the booth wore a green eyeshade and long black sleeve-protectors. The lights were dim and sort of flickering. Then I saw why: they were open-flame gas-lights.

There were brass spittoons on the floor, and across the station a glint of light caught my eye: a man was pulling a gold watch from his vest pocket. He snapped open the cover, glanced at his watch, and frowned. He wore a dirty hat, a black four-button suit with tiny lapels, and he had a big, black, handle-bar mustache. Then I looked around and saw that everyone in the station was dressed like 1890 something; I never saw so many beards, sideburns and fancy mustaches in my life. A woman walked in through the train gate; she wore a dress with leg-of-mutton sleeves and skirts to the top of her high-buttoned shoes. Back of her, out on the tracks, I caught a glimpse of a locomotive, a very small Currier & Ives locomotive with a funnel-shaped stack. And then I knew.

To make sure, I walked over to a newsboy and glanced at the stack of papers at his feet. It was the *World*; and the *World* hasn't been published for years. The lead story said something about President Cleveland. I've found that front page since, in the Public Library files, and it was printed 11 June, 1894.

I turned toward the ticket windows knowing that here—on the third level of Grand Central—I could buy tickets that would take Louisa and me anywhere in the United States we wanted to go, in the year 1894. And I wanted two tickets to Galesburg, Illinois.

Have you ever been there? It's a wonderful town still, with big old frame houses, huge lawns, and tremendous trees whose branches meet overhead and roof the streets. And in 1894, summer evenings were twice as long, and people sat out on their lawns, the men smoking cigars and talking quietly, the women waving palm-leaf fans, with the fireflies all around, in a peaceful world. To be back there with the First World War still twenty years off, and World War II over forty years in the future ... I wanted two tickets for that.

The clerk figured the fare—he glanced at my fancy hatband, but he figured the fare—and I had enough for two coach tickets, one way. But when I counted out the money and looked up, the clerk was staring at me. He nodded at the bills. 'That ain't money, mister,' he said, 'and if you're trying to skin me you won't get very far,' and he glanced at the cash drawer beside him. Of course the money was old-style bills, half again as big as the money we use nowadays, and different looking. I turned away and got out fast. There's nothing nice about jail, even in 1894.

And that was that. I left the same way I came, I suppose. Next day, during lunch hour, I drew $300 out of the bank, nearly all we had, and bought old-style currency (that *really* worried my psychiatrist friend). You can buy old money at almost any coin dealer's, but you have to pay a premium. My $300 bought less than $200 in old-style bills, but I didn't care; eggs were thirteen cents a dozen in 1894.

But I've never again found the corridor that leads to the third level at Grand Central Station, although I've tried often enough.

Louisa was pretty worried when I told her all this and didn't want me to look for the third level any more, and after a while I stopped; I went back to my stamps. But now we're *both* looking every weekend, because now we have proof that the third level is still there. My friend Sam Weiner disappeared! Nobody knew where, but I sort of suspected because Sam's a city boy, and I used to tell him about Galesburg—I went to school there—and he always said he liked the sound of the place. And that's where he is, all right. In 1894.

Because one night, fussing with my stamp collection, I found—well, do you know what a first-day cover is? When a new stamp is issued, stamp collectors buy some and use them to mail envelopes to themselves on the very first day of sale; and the postmark proves the date. The envelope is called a first-day cover. They're never opened; you just put blank paper in the envelope.

That night, among my oldest first-day covers, I found one that shouldn't have been there. But there it was. It was there because someone had mailed it to my grandfather at his home in Galesburg; that's what the address on the envelope said. And it had been there since 18 July 1894—the postmark showed that—yet I didn't remember it at all. The stamp was a six-cent, dull brown, with a picture of President Garfield. Naturally, when the envelope came to Grandad in the mail, it went right into his collection and stayed there—till I took it out and opened it.

The paper inside wasn't blank. It read:

> 941 Willard Street
> Galesburg, Illinois
> 18 July 1894

Charley:

I got to wishing you were right. Then I got to *believing* you were right. And, Charley, it's true. I found the third level! I've been here two weeks, and right now, down the street at the Dalys', someone is playing a piano, and they're all out on the front porch singing *Seeing Nellie Home*. And I'm invited over for lemonade. Come on back, Charley and Louisa. Keep looking till you find the third level! It's worth it, believe me!

The note was signed Sam.

At the stamp and coin store I go to, I found out that Sam bought $800 worth of old-style currency. That ought to set him up in a nice little hay, feed and grain business; he always said that's what he really wished he could do, and he certainly can't go back to his old business. Not in Galesburg, Illinois, in 1894. His old business? Why, Sam was my psychiatrist.

THE MAN WHO RODE
THE TRAINS

Paul A. Carter

Now we come to the last tale in this book and also, perhaps, to the very last train ever to run. It is set in the future and concerns the ultimate railway enthusiast who has wealth enough to follow his interest about the world as the number of functioning railways dwindles away as airlines and other forms of transport take over.

Wherever he goes there is always another passenger he has seen before, one whom he recognises, one whom he will come to know on the very last train.

I. Via N.Y.C.—B. & A.

THE FIRST TIME I saw the old man was during the Second World War.

We'd gotten on board the train for Boston as soon as it was made up, and so all of us had seats. By the time we pulled out of the LaSalle Street Station people were standing in the aisles braced against the swaying of the cars, or were sitting on their suitcases. We were a long time getting out of Chicago, and just when the crowd had begun to settle down for the journey the conductors came wedging through to check tickets and move people around. Right behind them came a brace of MP's asking to see the service-men's furlough and leave papers. Then from South Bend to Sandusky a coffee-and-sandwiches man rode the train, and added to the confusion as he ran back and forth to refill the pot or to break a large bill for change.

When the train started up or stopped suddenly, babies would wake up and howl. Many soldiers' wives were travelling, some alone and some with several cranky kids. The air was hot and smoky, and your hand came away from the windowsill smeared with coal dust.

I was not yet ten years old and loved every minute of it.

At Buffalo my father got up to give his seat to a lady who was soon going to have a baby. He said he was going back to the club car, but I think he probably stood up most of the night. Mother had given up trying to read the big book she'd brought along—I think it was *Joseph and His Brothers*—and put out the little reading light. Curled up on the seat next to her, by the window, I lay awake and watched the block-signals go from green to red as we passed them, and tried to hear the whistle blow over the racket the rest of the train was making.

After Rochester they turned out the overhead lights, two by two—I could hear the series of hard snaps as the porter threw the switches—leaving only a dim blue phosphorescence which in my imagination transformed the interior of the coach into an undersea grotto.

Lulled by the *chuck-a-chuck, chuck-a-chuck* that the wheel trucks used to make in those days before the continuous-welded rail, I fell asleep in spite of myself.

When I woke up I saw the old man.

Mother and the pregnant woman were sound asleep. We were in one of those upstate stations that passenger trains on the New York Central stopped at in the middle of the night, with names out of the ancient history books. Since the train had stopped moving you could hear the sounds a coachful of passengers made during the night— yawns, sighs, light snores and very quiet talking.

The conductor and brakesman were standing right beside me. The conductor's pencil-flashlight beam made a small bright spot against the blue gloom. He was shaking the shoulder of the passenger who sat across the aisle from us, slumped in his seat with his hat down over his face. As the man gradually sat up you could see there was a body under the massive head, not just a heap of rumpled clothes.

He was dressed in the kind of suit you used to find on the rack in Chicago pawnshops, suits which couldn't have held a press even when they were new. His face hung as loosely as the clothes, with long ears, hanging jowls, and deep pouchy Saint-Bernard-dog eyes. His hands were big and had been strong. His thin hair, waxen face and frayed collar were picked out by the dim light in various shades of grey. To a small boy an elderly man would have seemed as ancient as Methuselah, but by anybody's standards this one was very, very old.

The voice, when it came, was thick and unintelligible— not with the incoherence of drunkenness, nor of sleep, but simply of great age. It scared me a little, like the opening shots in a good horror movie.

The conductor was getting impatient. 'Where's your ticket?' he demanded, shaking the worn coatsleeve almost savagely. The old man felt slowly in one pocket after another, uncomprehending. The brakesman finally found the battered ticket, stuck in the man's greasy hatband.

The conductor squinted to look at it under his pencil-light. 'You've ridden right past it,' he said. 'You'll have to get off and take the next train back.'

'He can't,' said the brakesman. 'Number Twenty-One doesn't stop here.'

The conductor said a word that a little boy like me wasn't supposed to know. 'Go on up to the smoker,' he told the old man.

The aged passenger gathered himself together with infinite effort. He fetched down from the luggage rack a bulging and well-worn briefcase with part of one strap missing. That surprised me; even at my age I knew briefcases were associated with the prosperous classes. Then he took down an old brown paper sack and a cane. He had some difficulty with sorting out the sack and the cane and the briefcase and his hat, but nobody moved to help him with them.

Finally he tottered out into the aisle. The coach was less crowded than it had been in the daytime, and he made his way forward without any trouble. As the door at the front of the coach swung closed behind him the train gently began to move. The next thing I remembered was Dad shaking me awake in the grey dawn to go back and get in line for the diner.

II. Via B. & M.—M.E.C.

By the time I was riding home from college the trains were not so crowded. Right after the war the Maine Central bought a fleet of new stainless-steel coaches with foam-rubber upholstery, and so for a few years—until they stopped cleaning them—the five-and-a-half-hour run from Boston down to Bangor was almost a luxury. Instead of standing in the aisles you might have the car almost to yourself, for the first section of the Turnpike, which would take all the passenger traffic in that state away from the rails one day, was beginning to make itself felt. Of course when the colleges and universities let out for vacations it was more like the old times.

From Boston's North Station to the dingy terminal at the end of Exchange Street in Bangor was a five-and-a-half-hour run, but on this particular trip home it was taking me nearer nineteen. In those days when you were sitting alone in a coach seat and a good-looking woman walked into the car you played a little game with yourself, which began 'I hope she sits near me.' A game was all it ever amounted to, but the girl who got on in Portland had lovely shoulder-length hair and nice legs and a slow, natural smile, and this one time the improbable had happened. More surprising still, the next part of the fantasy had come true also: we talked, and found that we had read the same new books and some of the same old ones. (We didn't agree about Eisenhower, but you can't have everything.) When we stopped within sight of the handsome old Georgian brick campus where she went to college I'd gotten off the train with her, much to my own surprise.

That was how I came to be on the milk train for the rest of the run to Bangor. This was one of the pre-war coaches they'd taken off their better trains. It clashed and jolted and jerked, and it had glary overhead lights that couldn't be dimmed, and ancient plush seats that couldn't be kept clean. But I did not notice these things for at least an hour out of that station. I was aglow with Althea's laugh, and her vibrant body moving lithely with me on the dance floor, and her abandoned, open-mouthed kiss outside the depot just before the conductor of the night train shouted 'Board!'

Even on those lumpy seats I might have drifted off into

a fatigued and happy doze. But as the train rattled across a trestle the rear door of the coach opened with a crash. Staggering with the train's motion a passenger lurched in out of the roar from the vestibule, bracing himself on a stout cane. In the other outsized hand he clutched a shabby briefcase and an almost shapeless felt hat. He was baggy-trousered and lank-haired, and even before I saw his face I knew who it was.

With the same ponderous shuffle I remembered, the old man made his way to the centre of the car. (Did I imagine that he nodded to me as he passed?) He wore the same threadbare suit, or its mate, and he wheezed heavily as he came alongside my seat. He was even more ugly than I recalled, and he smelled. *It's not the same man*, I told myself in a rising of middle-class revulsion. The thrill of disgust passed as he moved on down the aisle, and as a humane undergraduate rationalist I felt a bit ashamed of myself.

He sat down far forward near the water cooler, and from time to time through a haze of half-sleep I saw him get up and fill a paper cup with what passed for water on a run-down passenger train. The joyous glow of my date earlier that evening had vanished and irrationally I blamed the loss on the old man.

I woke up when the train stopped in Northern Maine Junction. Biting cold air drifted in through the open door. The Ancient Mariner, as I caught myself calling him, was gone.

III. Via N.P.—C.B. & Q.

My wife and I had taken the children up into the Vista-Dome for the crossing of the Continental Divide. The train swung through the long switchbacks like a great grey-green snake, and the cars ahead of us successively ducked in and out behind dark crags that might have sheltered a whole tribe of Indians waiting in ambush. A Montana sunset flared behind the junipers and limber pines that jutted from the light snow cover. But scenery was not what Mark and Karen were up here for. Karen was charming a captive audience of adult strangers with all the concentration her one and a half years could muster, and Mark was up front near the Northern Pacific's traditional Yin-and-Yang symbol, playing astronaut.

Marjorie seemed to have everything under control, so I excused myself to go below for a moment. She smiled fondly at me as I started down the narrow carpeted stairs.

In the corridor below I saw a girl with hair like Althea's.

A discordant surge of vivid and disloyal emotion rose within me. I hadn't thought of her for years, but for one poignant instant something gripped me and said *Althea, Althea, I wish I had never left you.*

Shaken, for I loved my wife, I pushed the washroom door, and there, sitting on the red imitation-leather bench by the window, was an aged man in a tattered suit. He had a briefcase beside him with one strap missing, and a cane lay between his knees.

Twice could be a coincidence, or a mistake, I thought. *But three times?* The aversion I had felt the last time I had seen him had given place to a burning curiosity. I lingered at the washstand as long as I dared, studying him in the mirror. And then, as I turned to leave, he spoke in that thick and horrible voice, and what he said struck an icicle into my heart.

'Hello again, sonny.'

I must have cried out as I slammed the door behind me, for a porter stopped and asked if anything was wrong. 'No, nothing,' I said. Then I caught him by his white sleeve. 'Wait,' I said, and detained him while, with a thundering heart, I re-opened that metal door.

Of course, there was nobody in there.

IV. Via C.B. & Q.

It was practically a Toonerville Trolley that banged and swung its way through the red rimrock country north of Thermopolis—one coach, one Pullman, and half-a-dozen baggage-and-mail cars in one of the least comfortable and most scenic rides in America. I had a dull paper to read on a dull subject at a dull meeting the next day in Denver. But I also had a new camera, and the conductor indulged my latest enthusiasm. 'Those windows are pretty dirty,' he apologised, and then he invited me to stand in the vestibule and let me lean out the open half-door to get my pictures of the shadow-moulded hills as we raced through the Wind River canyon.

It was strictly against the rule, and the C.B. & Q. could have had his job for it. But that entire train of necessity had an informal air. Since it carried no diner it stopped for half an hour in a little mountain town while the thirty-odd passengers had their evening meal, and afterwards the conductor came through the coach and counted us, and would toot the whistle if there was anybody missing. On the way out of the café I bought a roll of film and some souvenir postcards, and when I had finished reloading the camera and looked up, he was sitting just across the aisle.

The other times I had known wonder, then revulsion, and finally terror. This time his presence struck me as comic. This local was a very local train indeed, and all afternoon long people who knew each other had been getting on or off and shouting their delighted greetings, at every all-but-deserted mail drop in northern Wyoming. Somehow it seemed appropriate that I should speak to the old man, in the same spirit of 'it's a small world'.

He was silent for so long after I spoke that I thought he did not know me. Perhaps it was not the same person after all. But the slow metabolic processes of immense age at last produced thought and speech, and he answered me. 'We've covered a lot of ground in thirty years,' he said. *And in the meantime men have gone to the moon*, I thought, with a sudden chill.

It was too late to back out of the conversation now. The heavy, hoarse voice steadily became easier to understand, as though it were thawing out after long disuse. He talked, fitfully and with silences filled by the motion of the train: I listened. He talked railroading, mostly, and on that subject I was impressed by the clarity and encyclopaedic scope of his old mind. About the man himself I learned nothing. About me, I uncomfortably felt he knew quite enough already.

When the train stopped in Casper at 10 p.m. I decided to splurge—or was it rationalised fear?—and go back into the Pullman car. The conductor sent me inside the station to make the arrangements. When I got back on board ten minutes later, I was almost sorry to find the old man gone.

V. Via U.P.—C.M.St.P. & P.

The Great Society's high-speed inter-city rapid transit, when it came, was a flash in the pan. The long retreat of the passenger trains became a rout, even on the trunk lines west of Chicago. Our family took to gambling for life on the highways, or to flying, like everybody else. But planes did get grounded sometimes, even after complete Centralised Traffic Control was extended to all the airways.

The dreaded telegram came, saying FATHER PASSED AWAY COME HOME AT ONCE LOVE MOTHER. Marjorie was ill; I had to go alone. And when my flight was forced down at Salt Lake City I took a cab all the way to Ogden and caught the next train. With luck, if that was the right word for it, I might yet make it back in time for the funeral.

By virtue of its geography the Overland Route was one of the last to go. And the Union Pacific lavished a care and attention on its dwindling supply of passenger equipment as if it had been a dying biological species. So I sat at a table in a diner which had been meticulously recreated in the high style of the Gilded Age, gas-lights and all. Outside the window the desolate sagebrush hills, which had driven so many transcontinental passengers to boredom and beyond, gave reassurance as they flowed past that some things in a world of war and social chaos and capricious death were never-changing.

I never expected to see the old man (Ancient Mariner? Flying Dutchman? Wandering Jew?) in a diner. The grime of years of train rides would stain its linen. And where, the skeptical side of me asked, would he get the money to pay for his meal? But he was there. He came in and sat down in the seat opposite me, with more vigorous motion than I had thought he had in him. 'Hello, young fellow,' he said in that mumbly voice, and at once began to talk. He was more unintelligible than ever, and made me strain to catch every word.

He talked of the famous gold spike at Promontory Point in 1869, and of John Wesley Powell's Grand Canyon expedition shoving off in its three boats from the temporary railroad bridge at Green River only a few weeks earlier. He described Indian raids and the slaughter of the buffalo. He mentioned Collis P. Huntington and Leland Stanford, Oakes Ames and the *Crédit Mobilier* and the Mulligan Letters. He spoke with a kind of groping verisimilitude, and the cold conviction grew within me: *this man had been riding on trains even then.*

The Negro waiter—the U.P. had had a first-class row with the Civil Rights Commission over retaining *that* tradition—brought us our menus, outsized 'souvenir' folders out of keeping with the rest of the spirit of that museum-piece of a car. I buried myself in mine, trying to get my whirling consciousness under control. When I put the menu down, no one was sitting in the chair across from me.

But the water glass at his place was half empty.

Droplets of rain spattered against the outside of the dining car window. The harsh dry lunar hills were cloaked in mantillas of mist.

VI. Via C.N.R

The grandchildren all understood that along with his other anachronisms Grampa was a nut on railroads. And the kindest thing my daughter Karen ever did for her father was to talk them, one summer, into humouring me. So we found ourselves steaming across the Canadian shield in western Ontario. Yes, steaming, for some official in the Canadian National Railways had foreseen that if they kept a few coal-fired locomotives in repair for a few more years there would be aging buffs like myself willing to pay handsomely for the privilege of riding behind one of them. This one had a powdered-coal stoker and a high-pressure boiler, and at every five-minute stop I hopped down and trudged forward through the cinders just to admire its great drivers and listen to the hiss of steam.

Those station stops were like frontier outposts in our own West before it was tamed: wooden false-fronted buildings, a general store with a sagging front porch, onlookers in Levis, even a few Sioux Indians. The population explosion had scarcely touched this part of Canada. On the long runs between these stations there was no sign of civilisation except the trestles we crossed and the tunnels we went through; they had long since taken down the telegraph wires. Sparkling cold blue water, unyielding grey-pink granite, and endless miles of pulpwood forest—in its own way it remained one of the wildest places in North America.

Karen's children, born and raised in urbanity, were alternately awed and bored by the sight. The one intrusion of the modern world came when a few troops just off manoeuvres boarded the train—rangy, sunburned men in full battle dress, Scots probably, and the biggest, toughest-looking soldiers I had ever seen. My grandson Jerry was delighted with them, and I thought with a pang of our Mark, so like him at that age, long dead now in a Chinese ambush far away.

I did not really think I would see the old man while travelling with members of my own family. The one exception had been triggered by a long-buried and guilty feeling about that girl in Maine, a fact which inclined me to doubt the reality of all the other episodes as well. I knew all about compensatory hallucination and projection and the difference between suppression and repression—who doesn't?—and after the encounter in that archaic U.P. dining car I had dusted off my college psych textbooks and read them.

The millions of dark points of spruce gave way to a mixed growth dominated by scruffy poplars. We were coming out towards the prairie, I realised with quiet, nostalgic regret; out of Winnipeg we would take a strato-flight. Then a giant hand slammed the front of the train.

The domino-wave of inertia swept back in a series of crashes that caught up with our car and shook it horribly. The force flung me across the space between the two Pullman seats and on top of Jerry. He yelled, once, more in fright than in pain, and then struggled to contain his sudden scare like a good little soldier.

White-faced, Karen rapidly and carefully checked out the four children one after the other, and found no injuries. I got to my feet with more security than I really felt; I was not yet ready to be considered ancient and fragile, I told myself, and before she could ask them of me I said the words to her: 'Are you all right?'

'Oh, Daddy.' Karen hadn't called me that since she was a little girl. I caught her and held her hard.

Behind us a woman was screaming, and there might have been a panic. But the two soldiers in the car quickly took charge. 'Stay on the train,' one of them said, in a tone that stopped the fight that was developing as men struggled to get out the narrow rear door. 'There's nothing out there but swamp. It's warm on board, there's food in the diner, and they'll send somebody out to fetch us eventually.'

The passengers began to settle down. The car was canted a little to one side, but it had not jumped the rails. I looked outside and saw a brakesman step down and start walking back along the tracks. And then, between the seats opposite me, a pile of suitcases and rumpled newspapers moved.

As I crossed the aisle I knew already whom I would find, sitting on the floor with his legs sprawled up across one green seat. I tugged and hauled at the old man in a fever, almost hysteria. 'Don't move him!' said Karen sharply.

I began to work more gently. He breathed, regularly and easily. 'He's not unconscious—he's *asleep*,' I heard myself whisper.

The old man seemed monstrously heavy. One of the soldiers gave me a hand and we sat him up on the Pullman seat. We put his hat and his cane and his briefcase beside him—both straps were gone now, I noticed, and he had tied it up with cords. As soon as we settled him his great head slumped on his dirty shirt-front. His breathing deepened into a ratchety snore.

In the process of evacuating the train, signing waivers of damage claims, and so on, of course I lost sight of him again. The Mounties and the reporters were interested in my story of the man who had slept through a train wreck, but nothing more was ever found out.

VII. Via *Trans-Siberian*

Shortly before May day in the year 2002, the last passenger

train in the Soviet Union rolled out of Gorki Station in Moscow, laden with foreigners. *Pravda,* nearing its centennial, poked editorial fun at this latest proof of capitalist decadence, but Intourist made a good thing out of this pilgrimage of the railroad buffs, and got a grand haul in dollars, francs, and marks. The comfortable old *wagon-lit*-type cars were jammed with my own countrymen, most of them red-faced Babbitts wise in their own conceit. Some of them carried tape recorders, as if the train noises could have been heard over their own carnival revelry.

If I had travelled so far to be among such men, a nagging voice inside me asked, wasn't I really one of them? I had my defenses ready—after Marjorie died I needed to do something, and so on—but all at once I got up abruptly and left that car. I knew that up forward there would be a third-class coach with wooden benches. It would be full of Russians, gathered around a samovar of steaming tea. Someone would have a balalaika, and they would be singing. No doubt Intourist had overseen *that* feature of the trip for our benefit also, but the thought of it made me feel better.

This time he came out of one of the *wagot-lit* compartment doors. The old man saw me at once, and to my astonishment spoke to me in throaty Russian. And this time I realised in a hideous flash of panic that I did not want to meet him again, ever. I whirled around, caught myself on a stanchion as the train lurched, and ran back the way I had come.

The train clicked along a steady twenty-five miles per hour. The roar in the vestibule as I opened and closed the red-starred doors only fanned my fear, for even over that roar I could hear the shuffling *slap-slap* of those big, flat feet. *He can't move as fast as that,* I prayed. *Can he?*

'Wait!' the thick voice cried, in English, as I slammed another door right in his wattled face. I bumped into a guard, beg-pardoned in my tourist phrase-book Russian, and managed to wriggle out of his grasp an instant before the old man ran into him.

'Tcherti,' the guard exclaimed. My heart thudded and my head constricted, and the doctor had warned me about

227

that, but I staggered on into the midst of my crowd of excursionists. Never in my life had I been so glad to see a bunch of loud-talking, back-slapping Americans.

The train was slowing. We were not yet out of suburbia, which had expanded rapidly in recent years at the expense of Muscovy's log-cabin villages, *kolkbozes*, and birch forests. With a shudder of relief I got off at that first station stop, managed to talk myself out of being detained for questoning, and caught the next bus back to Moscow.

VIII. Via *Zimbabwe People's Railway*

Now I can better understand some men's addiction to alcohol or gambling. I did not want to see the old man again, but I could not stay away from the trains.

I fought it. I went on ocean cruises, descended in a bathyscaphe, kept myself fit enough for tramps through Scotland and Wales. I even booked passage on a rocket to the moon. But my doctor grounded me, on account of sheer senescence, I suppose, and when he had finished his examination I knew what I had to do. For who can escape what has been his doom from the beginning?

After the Australians discontinued the excursions out of Darwin and Perth and Alice Springs, the only place where you could go to take the train was Africa. A conscientious young man in the American embassy in Cairo tried to talk me out of it. White men were still not welcome in some of those countries, he told me; only their still-urgent need to earn foreign exchange made it possible for a non-Negro American to travel through Black Africa to the Cape. And travel in Africa was more strenuous than in Europe or the States, even today. 'Especially for a man your age,' he wanted to add, but I stared him down. I could play the game of venerable curmudgeon putting down the young whipper-snapper when I wanted something badly enough.

'Very well,' he sighed at last. 'But south of Lake Nasser you're on your own.'

Africa is everything that Hemingway and Isak Dinesen and Stuart Cloete ever said it was, and more. I forgot the old man in the wonders of the veldt. The luminous air, that you find in only one continent in the world; the vast waves of high grasses, and the grand solitary trees; fleet zebras and *wildebeest* bounding away, and sometimes, when the train stopped for water and coal, the grave cough of a lion in the night.

Again as in my boyhood the train was filled with soldiers. But all these soldiers were black. There was rebellion somewhere beyond the Zambesi, and they were on their way to help put it down. The American consul had been wrong; the big, smiling men treated me kindly, if also with a little condescension.

Every hour I was consciously expecting to see the old man, and so he did not appear. What did appear was an angry buzzing single-engined airplane, probably the oldest flying craft in existence outside the Smithsonian. A startled giraffe bounded up out of the grass and raced away. The soldiers jumped into action as a sinister *rat-tat-tat* shattered the calm air, and then the train shook to a furious explosion.

That had been a near-miss; for it kept on going. Then the brakes screamed in agony; the train commandant must have had to flatten every wheel on the train. A soldier pushed me gently but quickly out of my seat and I understood why the coach windows had steel shutters on them. He pushed up the glass pan, swung the shutters to, poked his carbine through the embrasure and blazed away. 'Damn white bastards,' said the soldier. Then he flung a glance my way. 'Sorry, Pop. No offense,' he said, as he put his eye back to the sights and squeezed the trigger.

The other civilian passengers—a few Europeans, but mostly Chinese—were crouching out of harm's way. Through the open door at the end of the coach I saw a soldier gather his knees under him and jump. Something spanged against the shutter. This time there could be no question that it was safer to stay on the train! But I ran down the aisle—*lightly for a man pushing eighty*, I thought smugly—and followed the last soldier to the ground. He hit the dirt and came up shooting.

'No civilians off the train,' a noncom shouted. Then he recognised me, and shrugged. 'Okay, Pop, if you want to, but it's your funeral.'

Under covering fire from the windows a skirmish line deployed towards a thicket two hundred yards away. From the clump of thornbushes came an irregular stutter of small-arms fire. It sounded like everything from target pistols to shotguns. Several of the skirmishes stopped in their tracks and fell, but they took their losses and kept on moving. In a moment they would be within easy throwing range for grenades.

The plane cirled and came back at us, and from a flat car at the end of the train came the *thump-thump* of anti-aircraft. The ancient warplane snarled down so close I could see the pilot straighten up in surprise as ground fire found him. The machine gun chopped one terrible swath through those exposed troops, and they sprayed wildly as the plane skimmed over treetops out of control. One spent 30-cal. slug pinged against the side of the train right over my head. I was utterly unafraid, for by then I knew that I was not going to die on solid ground.

The plane crashed in a pillar of black smoke laced with roiling flame. By that time the soldiers were swarming over the white guerillas in that thicket and it was all over. They took no prisoners.

The first choppers arrived from Lusaka almost before the kites had begun to settle to their work. The Air Force lifted out the wounded first, then the foreign tourists. The troops would go on with the train, shooting their way into Bulawayo if necessary. But I knew they would still carry one civilian passenger with them.

As the helicopter carrying me beat the air over the battlefield, I saw a familiar figure padding thoughtfully past a strewn heap of the slain, toward the nearest car. His shabby suit was even more incongruous against the green of the veldt. As he swung himself on board, he—yes, merciful Heaven!—he turned his pasty face upward and waved.

My story is not yet told, for no man can write his own closing chapter. But I know that there will be one more train. And I know who will be on it, waiting.

And I know who he is, now.

ACKNOWLEDGEMENTS

The editor wishes to thank the following authors, or their executors or agents for permission to include copyright material in this book:

Mrs Sonia Rolt: 'The Garside Fell Disaster' © 1948, from *Sleep No More*
Harry Harrison: 'The Last Train' © 1976

Every effort has been made to trace the copyright holders of these stories. The editor offers his apologies in the event of any necessary acknowledgement being accidentally omitted.

STAR BOOKS BESTSELLERS

FICTION

WAR BRIDES	*Lois Battle*	£2.50 ☐
AGAINST ALL GODS	*Ashley Carter*	£1.95 ☐
THE STUD	*Jackie Collins*	£1.75 ☐
SLINKY JANE	*Catherine Cookson*	£1.35 ☐
THE OFFICERS' WIVES	*Thomas Fleming*	£2.75 ☐
THE CARDINAL SINS	*Andrew M. Greeley*	£1.95 ☐
WHISPERS	*Dean R. Koontz*	£1.95 ☐
LOVE BITES	*Molly Parkin*	£1.60 ☐
GHOSTS OF AFRICA	*William Stevenson*	£1.95 ☐

NON-FICTION

BLIND AMBITION	*John Dean*	£1.50 ☐
DEATH TRIALS	*Elwyn Jones*	£1.25 ☐
A WOMAN SPEAKS	*Anais Nin*	£1.60 ☐
I CAN HELP YOUR GAME	*Lee Trevino*	£1.60 ☐
TODAY'S THE DAY	*Jeremy Beadle*	£2.95 ☐

BIOGRAPHY

IT'S A FUNNY GAME	*Brian Johnston*	£1.95 ☐
WOODY ALLEN	*Gerald McKnight*	£1.75 ☐
PRINCESS GRACE	*Gwen Robyns*	£1.75 ☐
STEVE OVETT	*Simon Turnbull*	£1.80 ☐
EDDIE: MY LIFE, MY LOVES	*Eddie Fisher*	£2.50 ☐

STAR Books are obtainable from many booksellers and newsagents. If you have any difficulty tick the titles you want and fill in the form below.

Name_____

Address_____

_____

Send to: Star Books Cash Sales, P.O. Box 11, Falmouth, Cornwall. TR10 9EN.

Please send a cheque or postal order to the value of the cover price plus:
UK: 45p for the first book, 20p for the second book and 14p for each additional book ordered to the maximum charge of £1.63.

BFPO AND EIRE: 45p for the first book, 20p for the second book, 14p per copy for the next 7 books, thereafter 8p per book.

OVERSEAS: 75p for the first book and 21p per copy for each additional book.

While every effort is made to keep prices low, it is sometimes necessary to increase prices at short notice. Star Books reserve the right to show new retail prices on covers which may differ from those advertised in the text or elsewhere.

STAR BOOKS BESTSELLERS

THRILLERS

OUTRAGE	*Henry Denker*	£1.95 ☐
FLIGHT 902 IS DOWN	*H Fisherman &*	£1.95 ☐
	B. Schiff	
TRAITOR'S EXIT	*John Gardner*	£1.60 ☐
ATOM BOMB ANGEL	*Peter James*	£1.95 ☐
HAMMERED GOLD	*W.O. Johnson*	£1.95 ☐
DEBT OF HONOUR	*Adam Kennedy*	£1.95 ☐
THE FIRST DEADLY SIN	*Laurence Sanders*	£2.60 ☐
KING OF MONEY	*Jeremy Scott*	£1.95 ☐
DOG SOLDIERS	*Robert Stone*	£1.95 ☐

CHILLERS

SLUGS	*Shaun Hutson*	£1.60 ☐
THE SENTINEL	*Jeffrey Konvitz*	£1.65 ☐
OUIJA	*Andrew Laurance*	£1.50 ☐
HALLOWEEN III	*Jack Martin*	£1.80 ☐
PLAGUE	*Graham Masterton*	£1.80 ☐
MANITOU	*Graham Masterton*	£1.50 ☐
SATAN'S LOVE CHILD	*Brian McNaughton*	£1.35 ☐
DEAD AND BURIED	*Chelsea Quinn Yarbo*	£1.75 ☐

STAR Books are obtainable from many booksellers and newsagents. If you have any difficulty tick the titles you want and fill in the form below.

Name_____

Address_____

_____

Send to: Star Books Cash Sales, P.O. Box 11, Falmouth, Cornwall. TR10 9EN.

Please send a cheque or postal order to the value of the cover price plus:
UK: 45p for the first book, 20p for the second book and 14p for each additional book ordered to the maximum charge of £1.63.

BFPO and EIRE: 45p for the first book, 20p for the second book, 14p per copy for the next 7 books, thereafter 8p per book.

OVERSEAS: 75p for the first book and 21p per copy for each additional book.

While every effort is made to keep prices low, it is sometimes necessary to increase prices at short notice. Star Books reserve the right to show new retail prices on covers which may differ from those advertised in the text or elsewhere.